Thy Servant a Dog

Rudyard Kipling

DODO PRESS

CONTENTS:

'THY SERVANT A DOG'

PLEASE may I come in? I am Boots. I am son of Kildonan Brogue—Champion Reserve—V.H.C.—very fine dog; and no-dash-parlour-tricks, Master says, except I can sit-up, and put paws over nose. It is called 'Making Beseech.' Look! I do it out of own head. Not for telling... This is Flat-in-Town. I live here with Own God. I tell:

I

There is walk-in-Park-on-lead. There is off-lead-when-we-come-to-the- grass. There is 'nother dog, like me, off-lead. I say: 'Name?' He says: 'Slippers.' He says: 'Name?' I say: 'Boots.' He says: 'I am fine dog. I have Own God called Miss.' I say: 'I am very-fine dog. I have Own God called Master.' There is walk-round-on-toes. There is Scrap. There is Proper Whacking. Master says 'Sorry! Awfully sorry! All my fault.' Slippers's Miss says: 'Sorry! My fault too.' Master says: 'So glad it is both our faults. Nice little dog, Slippers.' Slippers's Miss says 'Do you really think so?' Then I made 'Beseech.' Slippers's Miss says: 'Darling little dog, Boots.' There is on-lead, again, and walking with Slippers behind both Own Gods, long times... Slippers is not-half-bad dog. Very like me. 'Make-fine-pair, Master says...There is more walkings in Park. There is Slippers and his Miss in that place, too. Own Gods walk together—like on-lead. We walk behind. We are tired. We yawn. Own Gods do not look. Own Gods do not hear...They have put white bows on our collars. We do not like. We have pulled off. They are bad to eat...

II

Now we live at Place-in-Country, next to Park, and plenty good smells. We are all here. Please look! I count paws. There is me, and own God- Master. There is Slippers, and Slippers's Own God-Missus. That is all my paws. There is Adar. There is Cookey. There is James-with-Kennel- that-Moves. There is Harry-with-Spade. That is all Slippers's paws. I cannot count more; but there is Maids, and

Odd-man, and Postey, and Telegrams, and Pleasm-butcher and People. And there is Kitchen Cat which runs up Wall. Bad! Bad! Bad!

At morning-time Adar unties and brushes. There is going quick upstairs past Cookey and asking Gods to come to brekker. There is lie-down- under-the-table-at-each-end, and heads-on-feets of Gods. Sometimes there is things-gived-under-table. But 'must never beg.'

After brekker, there is hunting Kitchen Cat all over garden to Wall. She climbs. We sit under and sing. There is waiting for Gods going walks. If it is nothing-on-their-tops, it is only round the garden, and 'get-off-the-flower-bedsyou-two!' If it is wet, it is hearth-rugs by fire, or 'who-said-you-could-sit-on-chairs-Little-Men?' It is always being-with Own Gods—Own Master and Own Missus. We are most fine dogs...There is Tall far-off dog, which comes through laurels, and looks. We have found him by own dust-bin. We said: 'Come back, and play!' But he wented off. His legs are all bendy. And wavy ears. But bigger than Me!

III

AUGUST 1923

Please sit up! I will tell you by Times and Long Times—each time at a time. I tell good things and dretful things.

Beginning of Times. There was walk with Own Gods, and 'basket-of-things-to-eat-when-wesit-down—piggies.' It were long walks. We ate lots. After, there was rabbits which would not stay. We hunted. We heard sorrowful singing in woods. We went look-see. There was that far-off Tall dog, singing to hole in bank. He said: 'I have been here dretful long whiles, and I do not know where here is.' We said 'Follow tails!' He followed back to Own Gods. Missus said: 'Oh, you poor big baby!' Master said: 'What on earth is Kent's puppy doing here?' Tall dog went on tum plenty, and said small. There was 'give-him-what's- left.' He kissed hands. We all wented home across fields. He said he were playing with washing-on-line, which waved like tails. He said little old dog with black teeth came, and said he would make him grow- into-a-hound, if he went with. So he wented with, and found beautiful Smell. Old dog said him to put his dash-nose-upon-the-ground and puzzle. He puzzled long ways with old dog. There was field full of 'ware-sheep and beautiful Smell stopped. Old dog was angry and said him to cast-forward. But Peoples came saying loud. He ran into woods. Old dog said if he waited long enough there he would grow-into-a- hound, and it would do-him-good to have to find his way home, because he would have to do it most of his life if he was so-dash-stoopid-as- all-that. Old dog went away and Tall dog waited for more beautiful Smell, and it was night-times, and he did not know where home was, and he singed what we heard. He were very sorry. He is quite new dog. He says he is called 'DamPuppy.' After long whiles there was smells which he knew. So he went through hedge and ran to his home. He said he was in-for-Proper-Whacking.

One Time after That. Kitchen Cat sits on Wall. We sing. She says: 'Own Gods are going away.' Slippers says: 'They come back at Biscuit-time.' Kitchen Cat says: 'This time they will go and never come back.' Slippers says: 'That is not real rat.' Kitchen Cat says: 'Go to top of House, and see what Adar is doing with kennels-that-shut.'

We go to top of House. There is Adar and kennels-that-shut. She fills with things off Gods' feets and tops and middles. We go downstairs. We do not understand...

Kitchen Cat sits on Wall and says: 'Now you have seen that Own Gods are going. Wait till kennels-that-shut are put behind kennel-that- moves, and Own Gods get in. Then you will know.' Slippers says: 'How do you know where that rat will run?' Kitchen Cat says 'Because I am Cat. You are Dog. When you have done things, you ask Own Gods if it is Whack or Pat. You crawl on turn. You say "Please, I will be good." What will you do when Own Gods go and never come back?' Slippers said: 'I will bite you when I catch you.' Kitchen Cat said: 'Grow legs!'

She ran down Wall and went to Kitchen. We came after. There was Cookey and broom. Kitchen Cat sat in window and said: 'Look at this Cookey. Sometimes this is thick Cookey; sometimes this is thin Cookey. But it is always my Cookey. I am never Cookey's Cat. But you must always have Own Gods with. Else you go bad. What will you do when Own Gods go away?' We were not comfy. We went inside House. We asked Own Gods not to go away and never come back. They did not understand...

IV

Time After. Own Gods have gone away in kennel-that-moves, with kennels-that-shut behind! Kennel came back at Biscuit-time, but no Gods. We went over House looking. Kitchen Cat said: 'Now you see!' We went to look everywhere. There was nothing...There is Peoples called Carpenters come. They are making a little House inside Big House. There is Postey talking to Adar. There is Pleasm-butcher talking to Cookey. There is everybody talking. Everybody says: 'Poor little chaps.' And goes away.

Some more Time. This night-time, Shiny Plate shined into our kennels, and made sing. We sang: 'When will Own Gods come back?' Adar looked out from high-up-above, and said 'Stop that, or I'll come down to you.' We were quiet, but Shiny Plate shined more. We singed 'We will be good when the Gods come back.' Adar came down. There was Whackings. We are poor little small dogs. We live in Outside Places. Nobody cares for.

V

Other more times. I have met that Tall far-off dog with large feet. He is not called 'DamPuppy.' He is called Ravager-son-of-Regan. He has no Own God because he will pass-the-bottle-round-and-grow-into-a-Hound. He lives across Park, at Walk, with dretful Peoples called Mister- Kent. I have wented to Walk. There were fine smells and pig-pups, and a bucket full of old things. Ravager said: 'Eat hearty!' He is nice dog. I ate lots. Ravager put his head through handle of bucket. It would not go away from him. He went back-first, singing. He sang: 'I am afraid.' Peoples came running. I went away. I wented into dark place called Dairy. There was butters and creams. People came. I went out of a little window. I sicked-up two times before I could run quick. I went to own kennel and lay down. That Peoples called Mister- Kent came afterwards. He said to Adar 'That little black beast is dam- thief.' Adar said 'Nonsense! He is asleep.' Slippers came and said: 'Come and play Rats.' I said: 'Go to Walk and play with Ravager.' Slippers wented. People thought Slippers was me. Slippers came home quick. I am very fine dog—but Master has not come back!

VI

After that Time. I am Bad Dog. I am Very Bad Dog. I am 'G'way-you- dirty-little-devil!' I found a Badness on the road. I liked it! I rolled in it! It were nice! I came home. There was Cookey and Adar. There was 'Don't;-you-come-anigh-me.' There was James-with-kennel- that-moves. There was: 'Come 'ere, you young pole-cat!' He picked up, and washed with soap, and sticky water out of kennel-that-moves rubbed into all my hairs. There was tieup. I smelled very bad to myself. Kitchen Cat came. I said: 'G'way! I am Filfy Bad Dog! I am Proper Stink-pot!' Kitchen Cat said 'That is not your own rat. You are bad because Own Gods do not come back. You are like Peoples who can not be good without Own Gods to pat.'

VII

Other Fresh Times. Now I am great friend of Ravager. Slippers and me have wented to hunt Hen at Walk. She were angry Hen-lady with pups. She bit Slippers, two times, with her nose, under his eye. We all went one way. There was Pig-lady with pups that way. We went other way. There was Mister-Kent-Peoples with whack-stick that way. We wented more ways, quick. We found a fish-head on a heap of nice old things. There was Ravager. We all went for play. There was cow-pups in field. They ran after. We went under gate and said. They ran away....an after till they stopped. They turned round. We went away again. They ran after. We played a long while. It were fun. Mister-Kent-People and more Peoples came calling dretful names. We said to Ravager: 'We will go home.' Ravager said:

'Me too.' He ran across field. We went home by small ditches. We played Rat-sticks on the lawn.

Cowman Peoples came and said to Adar 'Those two little devils have been chasing pounds off the calves!'Adar said: 'Be ashamed of yourself! Look at 'em! Good as gold!' We waited till Peoples were gone. We asked for sugar. Adar gave. Ravager came through laurels—all little. He said: 'I have had Proper Whacking. What did you get?' We said 'Sugar.' He said: 'You are very fine dogs. I am hungry.' I said: 'I will give you my store-bone in the border. Eat hearty.' He digged. We helped. Harry-with-Spade came. Ravager went through laurels like Kitchen Cat. We got Proper Whacking and tie-up for digging in borders ...When we are bad, there is Sugar. When we are good, there is Whack-whack. That is same rat going two wrong ways...

VIII

Harry-with-Spade has brought a Rat...Look, please! Please look! I am Rrreal Dog! I have killed a Rat. I have slew a Rat! He bit me on the nose. I bit him again. I bit him till he died. I shookened him dead! Harry said 'Go-ood boy! 'Born ratter!' I am very-fine-dog- indeed! Kitchen Cat sat on the Wall and said: 'That is not your own Rat. You killed it to please a God.' When my legs are grown, I will kill Kitchen Cat like Rats. Bad! Bad! Bad!

IX

Time soon After. I wented to Walk to tell my friend Ravagerabout my Rat, and find more things to kill. Ravager said: 'There is 'ware-sheep for me, and there is 'ware-chicken for me, but there is no 'ware-Bull for me. Come into Park and play with Bull-in-yard.' We went under Bull's gate in his yard. Ravager said 'He is too fat to run. Say!' I said. Bull said. Ravager said. Slippers said. I got under watertrough and said dretful things. Bull blew with nose. I went out through fence, and came back through another hole. Ravager said from other side of yard. Bull spun. He blew. He was too fat. It were fun. We heard Mister-Kent saying loud. We went home across Park.

Ravager says I am True Sporting Dog, only except because of my little legs.

X

OCTOBER 1923

Bad Times dead. Sit up! Sit up now! I tell! I tell! There has been washings and Sunday collars. Carpenter Peoples has gone away, and left new Small House inside Big House. There is very small kennel-that- rocks inside Small House. Adar showed. We went to James's house. He were gone away with kennel-that-moves. We went to front-gate. We heard! We saw! Own Gods—very Own Gods—Master—Missus—came back! We said. We danced. We rolled. We ran round. We went to tea, heads-on- feets of Own Gods! There were buttered toasts gived under table, and two sugars each...

We heard New Peoples talking in Big House. One Peoples said: 'Angh! Angh!' very small like cat-pups. Other Peoples said: 'Bye-loe! Bye- loe! 'We asked Own Gods to show. We went upstairs to Small House. Adar was giving cup-o'-tea to New Peoples, more thick than Adar, which was called 'Nurse.' There was very-small-talk inside kennel-that-rocks. It said 'Aie! Aie!' We looked in. Adar held collars. It were very Small Peoples. It opened its own mouth. But there was no teeth. It waved paw. I kissed. Slippers kissed. New Thick, which is that Nurse, said: 'Well-Mum-I-never!' Both Own Gods sat down by Smallest Peoples and said and said and kissed paw. Smallest Peoples said very loud. New Thick gave biscuit in a bottle. We tail-thumped on floor, but 'not- for-you-greedies.' We went down to hunt Kitchen Cat. She ran up apple—tree. We said 'Own Gods have come back, with one Smallest New Peoples, in smallest-kennel!' Kitchen Cat said: 'That is not Peoples. That is Own Gods' Very Own Smallest. Now you are only dirty little dogs. If you say too loud to me or Cookey, you will wake that Smallest, and there will be Proper Whackings. If you scratch, New Thick will say: "Fleas! Fleas!" and there will be more Proper Whackings. If you come in wet, you will give Smallest sneezes. So you will be pushed Outside, and you will scratch at doors that shut-in- your-eye. You will belong with Yards and Brooms and Cold Passages and all the Empty Places.' Slippers said: 'Let us go to Own Kennel and lie down.' We wented.

We heard Own Gods walking in garden. They said: ''Nice to be home again, but where are the Little Men?' Slippers said: 'Lie still, or they will push us into the Empty Places.' We lay still. Missus called: 'Where is Slippers?' Master called: 'Boots, you ruffian! Hi Boots!' We lay still. Own Gods came into yard and found. They said: 'Oh, there you are! Did you think we would forget you? Come-for-walks.' We came. We said soft. We rolled before feets, asking not to be pushed into Empty Places. I made a Beseech, because I were not comfy. Missus said: 'Who'd have thought they'd take it this way, poor Little Men?' Master threw plenty sticks. I picked up and brought back. Slippers went inside with Missus. He came out quick. He said: 'Hurry! Smallest is being washed.' I went like rabbits. Smallest was all no-things on top or feets or middle. Nurse, which is Thick, washed and rubbed, and put things on-all-over afterwards. I kissed hind-feet. Slippers too. Both Gods said 'Look—it tickles him! He laughs. He knows they're all right!' Then they said and they said and they kissed and they kissed it, and it was bye-loe—same as 'kennel-up'—and then dinner, and heads-on-feets under table, and lots things-passed-down. One were kidney, and two was cheeses. We are most fine dogs!

XI

MARCH 1924.

Very many Long Times after those Times. Both Gods have gone-week-ends in kennel-that-moves. But we are not afraid. They will come back. Slippers went up to talk to that Smallest and Nurse. I went to see my great friend Ravager at Walk, because I see him very often. There was new, old, small, white dog outside Barn. There was only one eye. He was dretful bitted all over. His teeth was black. He walked slow. He said: 'I am Pensioned Hunt Terrier! Behave, you lap-dog!' I was afraid of his oldness and his crossness. I went paws-up. I told about me and Slippers and Ravager. He said: 'I know that puppy. I taught him to grow-into-a-hound. I am more dash-old than

Royal, his grandfather.' I said: 'Is it good Rat? He is my friend. Will he grow-into-a-Hound?' Hunt Terrier said: 'That depends.' He scratched his dretful-bitted neck and looked me out of his eye. I did not feel comfy. I wented into Barn. There was Ravager on Barn floor and two Peoples. One was all white, except his black ends, which was called Moore. One was long, proper man, and nice, which was called m'Lord. Moore-man lifted Ravager's head and opened his mouth. Proper Man looked. Moore said 'Look, m'lord. He's swine-chopped.' Proper Man said: "Pity! He's by Romeo and Regan.' Moore-man said: 'Yes, and she's the wisest, worst- tempered bitch ever was.' Proper Man gave Ravager biscuit. Ravager stood up stiff on toes-very fine dog. Moore said: 'Romeo's shoulders. Regan's feet. It's a pity, m'lord.' Proper Man said: 'And Royal's depth. 'Great pity. I see. I'll give you the order about him to- morrow.'

They wented away. Ravager said: 'Now they will make me grow-into-a- Hound. I will be sent into Kennels, and schooled for cubbing-in- September.' He went after. Hunt Terrier came and showed black teeth. I said: 'What is "swine-chopped "?' He said: 'Being snipey-about-the nose, stoopid.' Then Moore came and put Hunt Terrier up on neck, same as Cookey carries Kitchen Cat. Hunt Terrier said: 'Never walk when you can ride at my time of life.' They wented away. Me too. But I were not comfy.

When I got home, Nurse and Adar and Cookey were in scullery, all saying loud about Slippers and Kitchen Cat and Smallest. Slippers were sitting in sink—bleedy. Adar turned sink-tap-water on his head. Slippers jumped down and ran. We hid in boot-house. Slippers said: 'I wented up to see that Smallest. He was bye-loe. I lay under Nurse's bed. She went down for cup-o'-tea. Kitchen Cat came and jumped into kennel-that-rocks, beside Smallest. I said: "G'out of this!" She said: "I will sleep here. It is warm." I said very loud. Kitchen Cat jumped out on floor. I bit her going to the door. She hit. I shook. We fell downstairs into Nurse. Kitchen Cat hit across face. I let go because I did not see. Kitchen Cat said, and Cookey picked up. I said, and Adar picked up, and put me on sink and poured water on bleedy eye. Then they all said. But I am quite well-dog, and it is not washing-day for me.' I said: 'Slippers, you are fine dog! I am afraid of Kitchen Cat.' Slippers said: 'Me too. But that time I was new dog inside-me. I were 'normous f'rocious big Hound! Now I am Slippers.'

I told about Ravager and Moore and Proper Man and Hunt Terrier and swine-chopped. Slippers said: 'I cannot see where that Rat will run. I smell it is bad rat. But I must watch my Smallest. It is your Rat to kill.'

XII

Next Time after Not-Comfy. Kitchen Cat is gone away and not come back. Kitchen is not nice to go in. I have went to see my friend Ravager at Walk. He were tied up. He sang sorrowful. He told dretful things. He said: 'When I were asleep last night, I grew-into-a-Hound—very fine Hound. I went sleep-hunting with 'nother Hound—lemon-and-white Hound. We sleep-hunted 'normous big Fox-Things all through Dark Covers. Then I fell in a pond. There was a heavy thing tied to my neck. I went down and down into pond till it was all dark. I were frightened and I unsleeped. Now I am not comfy.' I said: 'Why are you tied-up?' He said: 'Mister-Kent has tied me up to wait for Moore.' I said: 'That is not my Rat. I will ask Hunt Terrier.'

So I went back into Park. I were uncomfy in all my hairs because of my true friend Ravager. There were hedgehog in ditch. He rounded up. I said loud. Hunt Terrier came out of bushes and pushed him into a wetness. He unrounded. Hunt Terrier killed. I said: 'You are most wonderful, wise, strong, fine dog.' He said 'What bone do you want now, Snipey?' I said 'Tell me, what is "snipey-about-the-nose"?' He said: 'It is what they kill Hound puppies for, because they cannot eat fast or bite hard. It is being like your nose.' I said: 'I can eat and bite hard. I am son of Champion Kildonan Brogue—Reserve—V.H.C.— very-fine-dog.' Hunt Terrier said: 'I know that pack. They hunt fleas. What flea is biting you?' I said 'Ravager is uncomfy, and I am uncomfy of my friend Ravager.' He said: 'You are not so lap-dog as you look. Show me that puppy on the flags.' So I said about Ravager sleep- hunting and falling in pond, which he had told me when he were tied up. Hunt Terrier said 'Did he sleep-hunt with a lemon-and-white-bitch with a scar on her left jowl?' I said 'He said he hunted with 'nother Hound—lemon-and-white—but he did not say Lady-Hound or jowels. How did you know?' Hunt Terrier said: 'I knew last night. It will be dash- near-squeak for Ravager.'

Then we saw Moore on Tall Horse in Park. Hunt Terrier said: 'He is going to the Master for orders about Ravager. Run!' I were runnier than Hunt Terrier. He was rude. There was Big House in Park. There was garden and door at side. Moore went in. Hunt Terrier stayed to mind Horse, which was his Tall Friend. I saw Proper Man inside, which had been kind to Ravager at Walk. So I wented in, too. Proper Man said: 'What's this, Moore? 'Nother Hunt Terrier?' Moore said 'No, m'lord. It's that little black devil from The Place, that's always coming over to Kent's and misleading Ravager.' Proper Man said 'No getting away from Ravager this morning, it seems.' Moore said: 'No—nor last night either, m'lord.' Proper Man said: 'Yes, I heard her.' Moore said: 'I've come for orders about Ravager, m'lord.' Proper Man sat look-not- see—same as Master with pipe. I were not comfy. So I sat up on my end, and put paws over nose, and made a big Beseech. That is all I can. Proper Man looked and said: 'What? Are you in it too, you little oddity?' Hunt Terrier said outside: 'No dash-parlour-tricks in there! Come on out of it!' So I came out and helped mind Tall Horse.

After whiles, Moore came out, and picked up Hunt Terrier, and put him on front-saddle, and hurried. Hunt Terrier said rudenesses about my short legs. When we got to Walk, Moore said loud to Mister-Kent: 'It is all right.' Mister-Kent said: ''Glad of it. How did it come about?' Moore said: 'Regan saved him. She was howling cruel last night; and when his Lordship looked in this morning, she was all over him, playing the kitten and featherin' and pleadin'. She knew! He didn't say anything then, but he said to me just now: 'Ravager will be sent to Kennels with the young entry, and we'll hope his defect ain't-too- heredity.'

Mister-Kent untied. Ravager rolled and said and said and played with me. We played I were Fox-at-his-home-among-the-rocks, all round Pig- ladies-houses. I went to ground under hen-house. Hen-ladies said plenty. Hunt Terrier said if he had me for two seasons, he would make me earn-my-keep. But I would not like. I am afraid I would be put-in- ponds and sunk, because I am snipey-about-the-nose. But now I am comfy in all my hairs. I have ate grass and sicked up. I am happy dog.

XIII

EARLY APRIL 1924.

Most wonderful Times. We are fine dogs. There was Bell-Day, when Master comes black-all-over, and walks slow with shiny box on top and 'don't-you-play-with-my-brolly.' That is always Bell-Day Rat. Nurse put Smallest into push-kennel, and went for walk-in-Park. We went with, and ran, and said lots. We went by Walk all along railings of Park. Ravager heard. He said: 'I will come. My collar is too big.' He slipped collar and came with. That Smallest said loud and nice, and waved paw. Ravager looked into push-kennel and kissed Smallest on its face. Nurse shooed and wiped with hanky. Ravager said: 'Why am I "slobberybeast"? It is not 'ware-Smallest for me.'

We all walked across Park beside push-kennel. There was noise behind bushes. Bull-which-we-played-with-in-yard came out, and digged with paws and waved tail. Nurse said 'Oh, what shall I do—I do? My legs are wobbly.' She took Smallest out of push-kennel and ran to railings. Bull walked quick after. We ran in front. Slippers and I said lots. Ravager jumped at his nose and ran. Bull spun. Ravager ran behind push-kennel. Bull hit push-kennel on one side, and kneeled-down-on. Ravager jumped at his nose, and Slippers bit behind. Me too. Bull spun. Ravager ran a little in front. Bull came after to shrubbery. Ravager said: 'Chop him in cover!' We chopped, running in and out. Then Ravager bited and jumped back-with-barks before nose. It was fun. Bull got bleedy. Slippers and me said dretful things. Bull ran away into Park and stopped. We said from three places, so he could not choose which. It were great fun.

Peoples called out from railings round Walk. There was Nursey paws-up on ground, kicking feet. There was that Smallest and Own Gods holding tight. There was Mister-Kent-Peoples. Bull said, quite small—like cow-pup. Mister-Kent came and put stick at Bull's nose and took away on-lead. All the Peoples on the railing said most loud at us. We were frightened, because of chasing-pounds-off-those-calves. We went home other ways. Ravager came with, because he had slipped his collar and was in for Proper-Whack-Whack. I opened dust-bin with my nose-like I can do. There were porridge and herring-tails and outsides of cheeses. It was nice. Then Ravager stuck up his back-hairs most dretful, and said: 'If I am for Proper Whackings, I will chop Mister-Kent.' We went with to see.

There was plenty Peoples there, all Bell-Day-black all over. We saw Moore. We saw Mister-Kent. He was bleedy one side his blacks. He blew. He said 'Ravager's made a proper hash of him. Look at me Sunday-best!' Moore said: 'That shows he ain't swine-chopped to matter.' Mister-Kent said: 'Dam-all-how-it-shows! What about my Bull?' Moore said 'Put him down to the Poultry Fund; for if ever Bull cried dung-hill, he did with Ravager.' Mister-Kent said plenty-lots.

Ravager walked slow round barn and stopped stiff. His back-hairs was like angry Gentlemen-pigs. Mister-Kent began to say dretful. Moore said: 'Keep away. He has his mother's temper, and it's dash-awkward.' Then Moore said nice small things and patted. Ravager put his head on Moore's feets, and all his back-hairs lay down and was proper coat again. Moore took him to kennel, and filled water-trough, and turned straw on sleeping-bench. Ravager curled up like small puppy, and kissed hands. Moore said: 'Let him be till he sees fit to come out. Else there'll be more hurt than your Bull.'

Slippers and me ran away. We was afraid. We were dretful dirty. My nice frilly drawers was full of sticky burrs, and our front-shirts were bleedy off Bull. So we went to our Adar, but Own Gods and Smallest and Nurse Thick came, and they all said and said and petted, except Cookey because Kitchen Cat is not come back. There was wonderful things-under-table at dinner. One was liver. One was cheese- straw and one was sardine. Afterwards, was coffee-sugar. We wcnted up to see Smallest bye-loed. He is quite well. We are most fine dogs. Own Gods keep saying so. It are fun!

Just after that Times. There is no more Ravager at Walk. I have wented to see him. Moore came with Tall Horse and cracky-whip and took. Ravager showed very proud dog inside (he said), but outside frightened puppy. He said I were his true friend in spite of my little legs. He said he will come again when he is grown-into-a-Hound, and I will always be his True Small Friend. He went looking back, but Moore cracked whip. Ravager sung dretful. I heard him all down the lane after I could see. I am sorrowful dog, but I am always friend of my friend Ravager. Slippers came to meet me at Rabbit Holes. We got muddy on tum, because we have low clearances. So we went to our Adar for clean.

Kitchen Cat was on Wall again. Slippers said: 'Give her cold-dead-rat.' We wented-past-under quite still. She said: 'I am Kitchen Cat come back, silly little pups!' We did not say or look. We went to Adar. Slippers said me: 'Now we hunt Bulls in Parks, do not ever say to Kitchen Cat—ever!' I said: 'Good rat! You are wise dog.' Cookey picked up and said: 'Mee own precious Pussums!' Kitchen Cat said: 'I am Cat, not Dog, drat you!' Cookey kept on petting. Then she tied up by basket in kitchen, and said: 'Now you've had your lesson about going up to the nursery, you'll stay with me in future and behave!' Kitchen Cat spitted. Cookey took broom in case we hunted; but we went past quite still. This is finish to Kitchen Cat. We are fine dogs. We hunt Bulls. She does not hunt real rats. She is Bad! Bad! Bad!

XIV

LATE APRIL 1925

Most Wonderful Times. This is me—Boots. Three years old. I am 'sponsible dog (Slippers, too), Master says. We are 'sponsible for that Smallest. He can get out of push-kennel. He walks puppy-way between Slippers and me. He holds by ears and noses. When he sits down, he pulls up same way. He says: 'Boo-boo!' That is me. He says: 'See-see!' That is Slippers. He has bitted both our tails to make his teeth grow strong, because he has no bone at night. We did not say. He has come into both our kennels, and tried to eat our biscuit. Nurse found. There was smallest Whack-Whacks. He did not say. He is finest Smallest that is.

He had washings and new collar and extra brush. It was not Bell-Day. It was after last-run-of-season. He walked on lawn. We came, one each side. He held. There was horns in Park. I were tingly in all my hairs. But I did not say. ('Too old to make-fool-of-myself, my time of life, Master says.) There was Hounds and Pinks coming on grass. There was Moore—but he was Pinks. There was Mister-Kent. But he was like rat- catcher, Hunt Terrier said. There was nice Proper Man which was kind to Ravager in barn about being swine-chopped. There was some more Pinks, but not friends. Moore took all Hounds to gate by lawn. They sat down quiet. They was beautiful muddy, and seeds in coats and tails, and ears bleedy. Hunt Terrier sat in own basket on Tall Horse. When Moore put him down he said dretful things to Hounds. They did not say back. Proper Man said to Master and Missus: 'We have come to call with brush for that Smallest.'

Smallest liked because it tickled; but Nurse Thick washed off with hanky quick. Master-an'-Missus said: 'How did Ravager do?' Proper Man said: 'As usual. 'Led from end to end. He wants to talk to you.' Ravager stood up tall at the gate and put nose through. Smallest stretched out and Ravager kissed. Then Moore said: 'Over, lad!' Ravager overed in one jump, and said to Smallest, two times most loud, like Bell-Day, and played puppy very careful, and let Smallest hold by ears. His ears was all made round.

He spoke me. I went paws-up, because he were so big and dretful and strong. He said 'Drop it, Stoopid! 'Member me bein' lost? 'Member Bucket and Fishheads? 'Member Bull? 'Member Cow-pups and Lady-pigs and Mister-Kent and Proper Whackings and all those things at Walk? You are True Sporting Dog, except only because of your little legs, and always true friend of Ravager.' He rolled me over, and held down with paws, and play-bit in my neck. I play-bitted him too, right on jowels! All the Hounds saw! I walked round stiff-on-toes, most proud.

Then Hunt Terrier wiggled under gate without leave. Proper Man said to Missus: 'He is pensioned now, but it would break his heart not to turn out with the rest. He can't hurt your dogs, poor fellow.' Hunt Terrier walked-on-toes round me and showed black teeth. I went paws-up, because he were old and dretful about knowing Uncomfy things. He said: 'I will let you off this time, Snipey, because you knew about Ravager sleep-hunting in Dark Covers. 'Dash narrow shave, that! Now I must go and look after the young entry. Not one-dash-Hound among 'em!'

He went away and bitted at an old Lady-Hound, lemon-and-white, with black bites on jowels. She said, and wrinkled nose dretful, but she did not chop. She sat and looked at Ravager through gate, and said to him—like Bell-Day, but more loud. Proper Man said: 'Old Regan wants her tea. 'Fraid we must be going.' They wented away. There was horns and Horses and Pinks, and Hounds jumping up, and Moore saying names loud, and Ravager overed gate most beautiful. They wented all away— all—all. I were very small little dog.

Then Smallest said: 'Boo-boo!' 'See-see!' He took necks by collars. He said to Own Gods: 'Look! Look! Own 'ounds! Own 'ounds! Turn on tea, 'ounds.'...

THE GREAT PLAY HUNT

PLEASE! Door! Open Door!...This is me—Boots—which told you all those things about my true friend Ravager at Walk and Mister-Kent-Peoples and Kitchen Cat and Master-Missus and Smallest, when I were almost Pup. Now I am 'sponsible dog, rising eight. I know all about Peoples' talkings. No good saying r-a-t-s or w-a-l-k-s to me. I know! (Slippers too.)

Slippers is 'sponsible for Smallest, risen seven and a half, because Smallest belongs to Missus. And Slippers too. I help. It is very fine Smallest. It has sat on Tall Horse, which is called Magistrate, in front of that White Man which was kind to Ravager at Walk, which I told you, which is called Moore-Kennel-Huntsman. It has learned to keep hands down and bump, and fall off proper, and all those things. Now he has own pony called Taffy-was-a-Welshman. He rides with Moore and Magistrate all-over-Park. We come with. And he goes to Meet when it is at Kennels. Master-Missus say he must not real-hunt-just-yet. He does not like and says. I come to Meets with James in kennel-that- moves because of those dash new Hunt Terriers. I speak to my friend Ravager from next to steering-wheel, where I sit. He is best-hound- ever-was, Moore says. He walks close to near fore-leg of Magistrate. It is most 'sponsible place. He has nigh-half-choked Upstart for trying to take it, Moore says.

Now I will tell things and things like rats running.

First, 'was dash-bad business about Smallest in Old Nursery before brekker. There was hard tight collar. That new Nursey, which is called Guvvy, pinched under neck. Smallest said about boney old Lady-Hound. Guvvy said-and-said and shook Smallest. We shook too—one each side her middle dress. We did not nip. It tore of herself. Missus came up quick. Guvvy said all-about-all again. We wented downstairs quick. Missus called to Master. He said: 'Come here, you two sweeps!' There was Proper Whacking with own cutty-whip. But we did not nip that Guvvy. There was whack-whack for Smallest too. He was put in corner till 'I-am-sorry.' We went with to sit by, same as always with old Nursey. Missus said: 'I will not have my son's education perverted by two 'sreputable curs.' There was order not to be with Smallest all whole day. And nothing gived under-table at brekker. So we wented to dust-bin, which I can open with my nose. House not comfy because of Guvvy saying about us to our Adar. Our Adar said 'P'raps I ought to have warned you, but now you have had your lesson. Of course, Slippers will never forgive you for touching Master Digby, and as for that Boots, he can bear malice for months!' After dust-bin I said Slippers: 'Come for walk-about.' He said 'Own-God-Master always wants you help him walk-about after brekker.' I said: 'I do not want Own God. I did not nip that Guvvy-Lady-Hound. Come with.' Slippers said: 'They have put soap on my Smallest's teeth for badwording. He is kennelled up in Old Nursery. I will stay at home. P'raps he will wave me out of window.' So I took myselfs to Walk, where Mister-Kent-Peoples is. I were nice to Mister-Kent's two Frilly Smalls, which I know since they came. There was bread and butter and sugar. There was: 'Run along to school now, dearies.' I wented with to take care. There was lots more Smalls going to school, which I all knew. I ran sticks for them. There was two pieces gingerbread and two sweeties. Then I wented back to Walk because I were hungry. There was two hen-heads outside ferret- kennel box. They were nice. There was Lady-Hen in barn hatching eggs. They were good. There was Ben-sheep-dog, which was tied up because of meddy that morning. He had left his bone out too far. I took away to Mice-field where Wood's Edge comes down behind Walk. I caught four mices by jumping-on through grass. There was some of very old rabbit lying about. But bad fur. So I unhad all which was inside me, and wented into Woods for drink in Middle Ride. And sleeped. When I unsleeped, there was that old Fox which Ravager calls Tags, because he has very fine brush. He is dash-old but dash-wise, Ravager says. There was steel-trap on near-fore. He was biting-out foot. He said: 'If I am found like this, it is finish-for-me.' I said: 'There is no Meet to- day.' He said: 'Every day is Meet for that dash-Ben-cur-dog.' I said: 'Ben is tied up. He has took meddy.' Tags said: 'Then there is a chance.' He bited his foot, same as me with thorns. He bited off two toes, and licked and licked. He said: ''Serves me right for being dash-fool, my time-of-life.' He said it were two-nice-kind-ladies, long ways off, across railway line in Cotswold country (because Tags does not kill at home), which took hens to be killed in kennels-that- move, which had set trap under hen-house floor, with chicken which he could see. He tried to rake out. Trap caught two toes. He came home with—four miles—all through the night-times. He said he could not kill for himself for long whiles now, because of sore toes. I said: 'There is a big bone and four mices in Micefield, and some of old rabbit.' He said: 'Good enough! Tell Ravager I am as lame as trees. I am two toes short. I will lie up for rest of season. Then I will go to my-home-among-the-rocks-in-Wales, if I can keep living alive.'

I wented back to Walk, because I were hungry again. Ben said me lots about his bone. I said back. I danced. A Kent Frilly Small came and said: 'There is Boots playing so pretty with Ben. May I take him home, in case he will lose himself?' I were very nice. But first was tea in Kent-kitchen with Frilly Smalls—bread and hamjuice. Then I took that Frilly back careful to own back-door. Adar said: 'Lost? Him? Boots? Never, me dear!' Own Gods was at tea. But not Smallest. Slippers sat close by door making sorrowful sniffles which Own Gods do not like. (I helped.) Master said: 'Dash-it-all, if the house is to be run by this blackguard Trades Union of ours, accept it. Have Digby down!' Smallest came down to tea. We was all-over-him. There was tea-cake and two sugars and ginger-biscuits. Missus said: 'Do you think Boots spent the whole day looking for Smallest?' Master said: 'Not if I know Boots.' Own Gods began talking Master-Missus way. We wented to help Smallest kennel-up. I played smelling rats and looking rat-holes in Old Nursery. I ran about and growled dretful. Guvvy did not like because of her feet. But I did not ever nip that Guvvy—more than Tags ever killed at Walk. (Slippers too.) 'Was dash silly business for me afterwards—my time-o'-life. Guvvy told Missus about rat-holes. Missus told Master. Master told James to look and stop rat-holes. James told Old Nursery was tight as bottles everywhere. Adar said me in scullery after: 'Boots, you come along o' me.' I wented up with. I were not comfy. Adar said: 'Now you find those precious rat-holes of yours.' I played looky-sniffy hard. But it were play rat-holes. I went paws-up. Adar said: 'I thought so, you little devil!' She took by collar and rubbed nose hard in corner, same as if I were pup being taught House. I were very angry. I wented under bed. She pulled me out by tail. She said 'You black-hearted little villain! But I love yer for it!' And she kissed me same as Small Pup. I were dretful 'shamed. But I did not ever nip that Guvvy.

Now I tell new things. Please sit up!

There was plenty-rides always with Smallest and Moore in Park. Smallest wanted to real-hunt dretful bad, but Master-Missus said not- just-yet-awhile. Moore did not say except to James at Meet, when Smallest tried to quick-up that Taffy with safety-pin. Moore saw. He said James: 'My money is on the young entry.' I said Ravager all those things which Tags had told me about his sore toes. Ravager said: 'Tell Tags I am dash-sorry for him. He has given me as much as I could do for five seasons, and he was not chickens then. I hope he will lie-at- earth till leaves-on, because business is business.' Next whiles I was at Middle Ride I told Tags what Ravager had said. Tags said his toes was not so sore, and if it were early spring, he could keep living alive—somehow.

Time whiles after that, 'was Meet at Kennels. Master-Missus said Smallest could begin real-hunting at cubbing-times next September. Smallest was dretful good, and talked Master-Missus and Slippers how he would hunt, till bedtime. I told my friend Ravager all those things, when I speaked loud to him next Meet, before all the Hounds. He said: 'I will show that Smallest a thing or two when he comes up. He is keen-stuff.'

Time whiles after that, Shiny Plate got up strong, and made-sing. Adar looked out from high-up, and said: 'Quiet!' We played Rattle-chain round our kennels. Adar said: 'Drat!' She came and unloosed, like she always does when we do enough. We went for walk-abouts in Gardens and Orchard like we always do when she does. It were fun. Then we heard 'Lost Hound 'like long ways off, but not proper singing. We said: 'Who is? Come here.' It said: 'I do not know where "here" is. I do not see.' I said: 'That is Ravager. Rabbit it!' We rabbited through Orchard. There was Ravager. But he walked side-ways, head-twisty-very dretful. I said loud. He did not know. He said: 'I will go quick to Kennels.' But he went round and round. He said: ''Ware Kennel-that- Moves!' Slippers said: 'It is strange new 'stemper-dog inside Ravager. 'Same what Cookey gave me egg-an-brandy-for.' Ravager said: 'Where is my own place on the Bench?' But he bumped trees and twisted. We were afraid. We came each one side him. We came to own kennels...He fell down between. We licked his head because it were bleedy. After long whiles he said: 'Where is this?' We said: 'This is Boots and Slippers.' He tried to go away to Kennels. He could not lift. We lay close and licked and licked till Adar pulled back kitchen-curtains for brekker. We said. She came quick. (Cookey too.) There was egg-an- brandy, as-fast-as-you-can. Master-Missus and Smallest came quick after. James went in Kennel-that-Moves to get Vet-Peoples out-of-bed- by-his-hair. Moore and Magistrate came quick too, because Ravager had not cast-up at Kennels last night, and Upstart had fought Egoist for Ravager's place on sleepy-bench, and Kennels was all-of-a-nuproar. Moore said small to Ravager, but Ravager did not say back. Moore and Master put him on potting-bench in shed after Harry-with-Spade had broomed out and got small stove lighted. Smallest was took away to brekker, saying loud. Vet-Peoples did dretful things to Ravager's head. There was put-him-to-bed after. Moore set away straw same as at Kennels. Ravager tail-thumped two small times. We was let lie. We licked and we licked his head. Vet said he had lost one eye for always and not-much-chance for other. He said it were some-dash-motor. And Ravager were sick dog!

All those whiles, Smallest came to sit with, 'cept only when Guvvy took away, or it was rides in Park. Me too, except if Master wanted me help him walk-about farms. One time I saw Tags in Wood Edge. I told about Ravager. He said: 'I knew it the same night. It were that kennel-that-moves of the nice-kind-ladies in the Cotswold country, which takes hens to be killed. Tell Ravager I am dash-sorry; because eyes are worse than legs. Tell him to come over some day when it is leaves-on, and we will talk old runs. We are both finished now; and no-bad-feelings.' And he said: 'Licking is best for cuts. Look at my toes!' And he said he was killing again off nice-kind-hen-killer-ladies, which was sending bill to the Cotswold and Heythrop. He said they was Prize Cockerels, but it were dash-difficult to get bellyful these hard late frosts. I said: 'There is fine dust-bin at our place. I can lift lid with nose. We will not tell.' Tags said me: 'If your legs was good as your heart, I could not live for three fields in front of you. I am ashamed—'my-timeof-life—to go dust-binning. But I will come. Tell Ravager not to make a song about it, if he winds me.' So he came to our dust-bin all quiet.

Whiles after that, Ravager was unsick Hound again. He said he had had thorn in foot at end of that run. He turned out on grass to bite it out, by gate of nice-kind-ladies where Tags killed chickens. Ladies was taking hens to be killed, lots-and-plenty, in kennel-that-moves. They skidded kennel on grass because they talked. They hit him into ditch, and he was made into strange blind dog. I told him about Tags and dust-bin. He said: 'That is all proper. Tell him to come and talk me old runs together, because we are both out-of-it now.'

Time whiles after that, Ravager got down off bench and ate grass. He said me: 'I will go to my Kennels and speak them all there. Come with, because I do not see except my near side, and dash-little there.' Slippers said: 'It is riding-times for my Smallest. I will wait.' So I wented with Ravager. I put me his off-side in case if he bumped. We wented slow up middle of Park, which he knew by nose. Kennels was shut. Moore and Magistrate was coming to take Smallest for ride. Proper Man were there too, with new-four-year-old. I sat down outside, because I do not like those dash new Hunt Terriers. Ravager put up nose and said very long at Kennel Gates. There was dretful noise inside Kennels, all together, one time, and stop. Proper Man said Moore: 'I did not think this would have to happen.' Moore said: 'I saw it once when I was stable-boy to the Marquis, me Lord.' Proper Man said: 'Let him in and get it over, 'Pity's sake!' Ravager was let go in. He went to window looking into Hounds' sleepy-bench. He lifted himself up slow on sill, and looked them with his near eye. He did not say. There was one time more dretful noise inside, together, and stop. Then he did say very long, same as Lost Hound. Then he looked in, and 'was one more dretful cry inside. He dropped down. He came out. I said: 'What is?' He said: 'Upstart has my place on bench. I will go riding with Smallest.' Proper Man said Moore: 'Come on!' But Magistrate's girths was slack. Moore tighted up very careful. Proper Man blew his nose angry and said: 'You are as big dash-fool as your Master.' We wented back to Smallest. Proper Man told Smallest Ravager would not ever come to Kennels any more, and gave him for very own to keep always. Master-Missus put in old Labrador Kennels by vegetable gardens, with day-and-night-bench, but never locked, so he could come and go like-he-felt. (I can open that with my nose too.)

After that, 'was plenty ridings in Park, because Magistrate had thick-leg and wanted gentle-summer-exercise. Those times, Smallest said all about real-hunting, same as always. Moore said, if Ravager could speak, he could show Smallest more than Master-or-Me. He said all about real-hunts and Ravager, and Romeo and Regan, and Royal and Rachel, and Rupert and Ristori, which was all Ravager's fathers and mothers; and Foxes and Scents and casting hounds, and those fine things. Smallest found small red rumpet in Old Nursery, and played it were Horn-on-a-fine-hunting-morn. Moore showed how to squeak with. Ravager showed Slippers and me how to answer to Horn same as Sporting Pack. It were fun.

'Was one time when leaves-was-all-on, Shiny Plate came up strong and made-sing. We played Rattle-chain till Adar loosed, like she always does. We went to see Ravager, like we always do then. 'Was Tags outside old Labrador Kennels down-wind under gooseberries, like he does when he comes for talk. There was big say-and-say about old runs with Ravager and Tags. They did not say same about things. Slippers said 'No use worrying dead rats.' Ravager said 'Better worrying dead rats than no rats ever.' Slippers said: 'I know a good rat. Make a new run by your two selves. Make a run for my Smallest.' Ravager said: 'He will come up with the young entry for cubbing in September. He will learn soon enough then.' Slippers said: 'But show him a run now by yourselves; because you and Tags are dash-cunning at both ends of the game.' Tags said: 'That looks like sound Rabbit. Bolt him.' Slippers said: 'Make my Smallest a play-hunt up and down Wood Edge Rides. That Taffy is all grass-belly. He cannot jump, but he can wiggle through anywhere. Make a play-hunt up and down all Wood Rides.' I said: 'And across Park, and plenty checks for me to keep with Ravager in case if he bumps.'

Ravager said: 'I will not bump. I know every inch of the Park by nose. I will not bump.' Tags said: 'I am lame. I am fat. I am soon going to Brecknock.' Ravager said: 'You are too much dust-bin. 'Do you good to have a spin in the open before you leave. 'Do us both good.' Tags said: 'That is Shiny-Plate-talk.' But he waggled his brush. Ravager said: 'What about scent this time-of-year?' Slippers said: 'Make it point-to-point, same as Hunt Races, and dash-all- scents.' Ravager said: 'But I must show our Smallest how proper hounds work. He must see a-little-bit-of-all-sorts.' Tags said: 'My toes tell me that when Shiny Plate sits down this morning, rain will come, and scent will lie.' Ravager said: 'You ought to know. Now, worry out run for Smallest.' So there were proper worry—like all shaking same rat— abour line-of-country for Smallest's play-hunt. It were across Park from Wood's Edge Rides by Cattle Lodge and Little Water to Starling Wood, and saying good-bye to all kind friends at The Kennels, and finish at Made Earths by Stone Wall on County road, because, Tags said, that were his back-door to the Berkeley Country for Wales. Slippers and me helped lots. Then rain came, like Tags' toes said.

Morning-time 'was finished raining. Moore came with Magistrate—which had thick-leg and smelly bandage—only-for-gentle-work. Smallest took rumpet with, and own cracky whip, same as always. Ravager ran near- side Taffy. Me too. We wented up by Micefields to Middle Ride because of soft going, Moore said. In Middle Ride 'was Tags waiting like he said he would. Moore said: 'Dash his impertininces! Look at him!' Ravager gave tongue and wented up Ride. Me too. Smallest sticked hand behind ear and squealed proper. Tags scuttled limpity, but dash-quick. Magistrate see-sawed like that thing in Old Nursery. Moore said: ''Old 'ard, you silly summer-fool, you! Come back, Master Digby!' Smallest said: 'Hike to Ravager Forrard on!' We rabbited down Middle Ride—- 'normous long way. Tags turned right-handed into cover at Keeper's Oak, so he could slip into Park by Beech Hedge Gaps and Three Oaks, like he said he would. It were thick cover. We took it easy because it were hot. I keeped beside Ravager because he did not see. Tags said him in cover: 'There is nothing wrong with your legs.' Ravager said: ''Sorry if I pressed! I know Middle Ride by nose. That were not bad beginning.' Moore said loud: 'Come away, Master Digby. You won't see any more of him. He'll be through all manner of counties by now.' Smallest said: 'Don't you hunt my hounds!' Taffy pecked on ant-hill in fern. Smallest pitched forward, and hit face on Taffy's head. His nose bleeded plenty. He wiped with hand across. Moore said: 'What will I say to your Ma?' Slippers said: 'Ravager, draw down West Ride, where that Taffy can see his stoopid feet!' Ravager spoke, and drew down West Ride over turf all proper, to Beech Hedge Gaps into Park by Three Oaks. Taffy wiggled through. Magistrate after. He were like bullocks. Moore was all leafy. He bad-worded Magistrate. Tags came out from behind Three Oaks like he said he would, and wented down Little Water. Smallest rumpeted. Moore said: 'He ain't ever going to cross the Park? Or is he? Dash if I make-it-out-at-all!' Tags went by Little Water to Park Dingle. He crossed Water two times, like he said he would, and went along from Park Dingle to Larch Copse.

Ravager took up scent and worked along Little Water quite slow, to show Smallest proper-good-work. Moore said: 'Watch, Master Digby! You'll never see anything prettier in your life—young as you are!' It were dretful strong scent. Slippers and me spoke to it loud. Ravager too. When we came to Larch Copse, where Tags had doubled, like he said he would, Ravager said: 'Stop it, stoopids! We lose the Scent here.' He threw up head, and went back to Taffy and Smallest, and sat down and scratched ear. (Slippers and me too.) Smallest said: 'Shall I cast them?' Moore said: ''Can't have it both ways, Master Digby. They're your 'ounds, not mine.' Smallest put finger in mouth and bited, like he does when he does not know. Moore did not say. We did not say. After whiles (we did not say) Smallest rumpeted, and cast back other side Little Water to Park Dingle. Ravager said: 'Our Smallest is no fool!' We all worked hard on back-cast. Slippers said: 'May I give tongue now for my Smallest? Scent is strong enough to kill pigs.' So he were let give tongue. (Me too.) Ravager confirmed. Tags got out of Park Dingle like he said he would. We all rabbited for Cattle Lodge in Park, where once fat Bull was which we hunted. It were sound turf which Ravager knew by nose. That were Frocious Burst. I led Slippers to Lodge. Tags got under yard-gate. Ravager said me: 'May I fly cattle-bars? I think the top one is down.' I said: 'It is up. Go under!' He were dretful ashamed, but he did go under. We all sat in calf-shed, where water-trough is, and drinked. We were thirsty. After whiles, Moore said to Smallest outside: 'What made you cast back at Larch Copse, sir?' Smallest said: 'If I were lame Fox pushed out of my Woods, I would try to get back.' Moore said: ''Eaven be praised! You have it in you! I 'ave only 'elped fetch it out!' Tags said Ravager: 'It is time I left the country. Was anything wrong with my double? Did either you little 'uns give that cub of yours a lead about it?' Slippers said: 'I did try to help my Smallest by edging off. But he was angry, and told me off proper. That back-cast were all his own rat.' Then Tags said Ravager: 'Why did you run so mute down Little Water? Young 'uns are always keen on music, you know.' Ravager said: 'Sorry! That was my Mother's fault, too, on a scent. She always preferred her work to her company. Same as me.' Tags said: 'Come on, then. Next point is Starling Wood. I shall work down old Drainage Ditch, taking it easy, and slip in by Duck's Hollow. It will be more little-bit-of-all-sorts for your Smallest.'

Tags broke to view behind Cattle Lodge, like he said he would. There were scurry over turf to Old Ditch. He dropped in. It were deep—with brambles. We took it easy. Smallest said loud, because he could not see. Moore said: 'They are working their hearts out for you in there, Master Digby. Don't press 'em. Don't press!' Ravager said Tags: 'Show a bit, now and then. The Young Entry are all for blood, you know.' So Tags showed up two-three-times edge of ditch. And Smallest squealed and was happy-pup. At Ditch-end Tags said: 'Come through Duck's Hollow quiet, and 'ware new hurdles.' So we did. Starling Wood was hurdled tight. Ravager took hurdles flying skew-ways, because he saw them a little. I were uncomfy of my friend Ravager. I did not know what he would fall on—same as me with lawnmower and the pheasant-bird. But it were only thistles. He said: 'Sorry! I forgot I were blind dog.'

We all sat. It were stinky, eggy, feathery birdy place—all sticks. Ravager said Tags: 'Moore never puts hounds in here. We do not like it, and Scent don't lie.' Tags said: 'But Moore does, and Foxes cannot be dash-particular.' Moore and Smallest came riding outside. We sat still. Moore said: 'He can't be there, Master Digby! No fox uses where starlings use. The Hounds won't look at Starling Wood.' Smallest said: 'You said hunting is what-can't-happen happenin' dash-always.' Moore said: 'Yes, but he's gone on to make his point across the Park. Come 'ome and wash your face 'fore any one sees.' Smallest said: 'And lose my Fox?' Moore said: 'Then get 'old of 'em and cast forward.' Smallest did not say. He took rumpet off his saddle and held out to Moore. Moore would not take. He wented over all red in his face. He said: 'I most 'umbly apologise, Master Digby. I do indeed.' Slippers said: 'I do not know this rat.' Ravager said: 'He is giving his horn to Moore, because Moore knows so dash-well how to find his fox.' Tags said Ravager: ''Better speak a little, or Moore will lose me—same as last season.' Ravager speaked. Smallest said: 'He is there! Ravager can't lie. You said so yourself. Get down-wind quick!' Moore wented. He hit Magistrate proper. Slippers said: 'Why did Moore not take my Smallest's rumpet?' Ravager said: 'Moore is too dash-ashamed of himself for trying to hunt another man's hounds—same as that snipey- nose-man which The Master gave his horn to, because he said he was whip to the Bathsheba Lady-Pack.' Tags said Slippers: 'Come with! Here is another bit-of-all-sorts for your Smallest.' They wented where wood was stinkiest. Big cub ran out under hurdles at Smallest. Slippers after. Smallest did not like. He said: 'Fresh fox! 'Ware cub! Hike back to Ravager, you dash-lap-dog!' And cut at Slippers with cracky- whip. And hit. Slippers came back quick. He said Tags had said him to- push-out-that-youngster-and-see-how-Smallest-took-it. Moore came round cover. Smallest said: 'I have bad-worded Slippers. I have cut at my own Slippers!' Moore said: 'Don't take that to heart! You can bad-word every one at cover-side 'cept your own Pa-an-Ma and The-Master-an-Me.' Tags said: 'I think I will start for Fan Dringarth to-night. This is going to be dash-poor country for cripples next season.' Ravager said: 'Have a heart! Stay and keep me company.' Tags said: 'I would, but I have only one brush. Now, next point is Made Earths at Stone Wall on County road, where I go under for Dean Forest. Ravager said: 'Made Earths is tight as drainpipes. You cannot get-away-out-of till dark.' Tags said: 'Drain-pipes heave in frost. Then Badgers work 'em. But first we say farewell to all kind friends at The Kennels. There will be check at New Firs. You little 'uns drop out there, and take it easy up to Fir Knoll, till we come back from Long Dip. Then join in for rattling finish.'

Slippers said: 'That Taffy cannot gallop to keep himself warm.' Ravager said: 'But Magistrate wants three-new-legs. We will take care of them. Now play proper Pack. Get away together!'

Tags broke under Taffy's nose. 'Was most beautiful cry, and Adar could have covered with sheets. After that I were not so quick as Ravager. It were falling ground and sound turf, which Ravager knew by nose. 'Was nice check at New Firs, like Tags said. Slippers and me dropped out. Presently whiles, Tags broke to view down Long Dip. Ravager on his brush. It were real business. Slippers and me wented to Fir Knoll and watched. Taffy and Smallest was littler and littler in Long Dip. Moore and Magistrate too. Tags and Ravager was littlest, farthest ways off, by Summer Kennels Yard. We heard Ravager speak most beautiful outside there. 'Was dretful common noises in Summer Kennels—like common dogs which cannot hunt when they want. I were happy-dog, because I do not like Upstart and Egoist. Nor new Hunt Terriers. (Slippers too.) We danced and singed.

Presently after whiles, Tags came up from Long Dip to Fir Knoll, dragging brush very limpity. He said: 'I am Sinking Fox! Ravager is Lost Hound! Taffy is cooked! Magistrate is fit-to-boil! Come along, little 'uns, and Devil-take-short-legs!' We rabbited. That were t'rific Burst. I headed Ravager for little whiles. We came to Made Earths screaming for blood. Tags got to ground in front of Ravager's front-teeth which was like rat-traps. We all wented singing down into the dark. We sat, tongues-out. Ravager said: 'Top-hole finish!' Tags said: 'Not bad, our-time-of-life. That last point was quite a mile.' Ravager said: 'I make the run four mile from start to finish. You are too good for those Welshmen. Keep with us.' Tags said: 'Not with that youngster coming on. But he is Sportsman. Hark to him!' 'Was Smallest outside and Taffy blowing. Smallest said loud 'He were lame! Don't let them get him! He are lame! Call 'em off, Moore, an' we'll look for that dash-cub.' And he rumpeted plenty. Moore said: 'We 'ave done enough for one July day, Master Digby. 'Ere's 'is Lordship coming, and I'll never 'ear the last of it.' Tags said Ravager:

'I think you will be wanted for hunting out of season. I am going to Wales. You are true Sporting Lot.' And Tags backed into Made Earths, which are his road to his home-among-the-rocks, where drain-tiles was heaved up and Badgers helped, like he said he would, till we could not see his eye-shine any more. Ravager called after: 'You are best of them all, Tags!' But Tags did not say back.

We wented outside. There was Proper Man on Tall Horse coming slow from Kennels. Ravager said: 'He is not our Master now. Play proper Pack.' We lay down round Taffy, which was shaking tail, and girths-loosed, and Smallest making-much-of. Ravager did head-on-paws, and looked Smallest. I did thorn-in-foot. Slippers did burrs-in-tail. Moore did feeling Magistrate's thick-leg, and brushing leaves out of his front. Proper Man came up slow. He took off cap to Smallest. He said: 'Bowfront Hunt, I presume. 'Trust your Grace is satisfied with amnities of my country.' Smallest said: ''Gone to ground. But it were spiffing run. I hunted own hounds. Listen, Uncle!' And he said and he said, like he can, about things, from find-to-finish. Proper Man said Moore: 'When you have quite done bot'nizing all over your belly, p'raps you will let me know.' Moore said: 'My fault, me Lord. All my fault. I 'aven't a shadow of an excuse. I was whip to one lame fox, one blind 'ound, two lap-dogs, and a baby! And it was the run of me life. A bit-of-all-sorts, as you might say, me Lord, laid out as if it was meant to show Master Digby multum-in-parvo, so to speak. And may I never 'unt again, me Lord, if it 'asn't made 'im!' Proper Man said: 'Let's have every last yard of it.' Moore said and said: Smallest said and said, all one piece mixed. Proper Man asked about Tags' double, and Smallest's back-cast, and Scent and Starling Wood, and all those things, lots-and-plenty. He said it were babes-and-sucklings. We did not say. We tail-thumped when names was said, but no dash-parlour- tricks. We was proper Pack.

'Middle of say-so, Kennel-that-Moves came down County road with Missus, which had been shoppings. She stopped and overed wall in one. She came quick. She said: 'Digby! Look at your face!' Smallest said: 'Oh, I forgot, Taffy pecked and pitched me forward.' She said: 'In you get with me, and have it washed off.' Smallest said: 'Oh,

Uncle!' Proper Man said: Let him take his hounds home, Polly. He has earned it.' Missus said: 'Then I will take Boots and Slippers. They don't hunt.' But we would not. She said. James said. Smallest did not say. So we would not go in Kennel-that-Moves. We wented all across Park with Ravager and Smallest and Taffy and Moore and Magistrate and Proper Man to Own Kennels-like proper Pack.

Please, that is finish for now of all about me-and-Slippers. I make Beseech!

TOBY DOG

PLEASE, this is only me-by-selfs. This is Boots which were friend of Ravager. I make Beseech...I tell. But I do not understand.

'Was time when Smallest went to Flat-in-Town for things-in-throat, which Vet-People cut out so he could sleep shut-mouth, and not ever catch cold. He said he would be dretful-good if we came after. So we wented with our Adar in dog-box-in-train. Guard People said we was Perfect Gentlemen.

Flat-in-Town were stinky. Smallest were sick-abed. Times after, he lay on couch-by-window-at-back which looks into garage-place. We sat in window because of cats.

One time 'was whistle-squeaky noises, and Frill Box, with legs under, came into garage-place. 'Was dog, like me and Slippers, with frilly collar. Plenty Smalls followed-tail. We told Smallest. He came to window in one. He said: 'Hooray; Punch-and-Judy!' Dirty Man, which was legs, came out from under Frill Box, and whistle-squeaked with things in front of teeth. Frill Dog walked with behind-legs and shaked hands with Smalls like Dirty Man told. Dirty Man went into Frill Box. Dollies came up on little sleepy-bench in front. One were all nose and bendy-back like which Smallest took off a Shiny-tree when he were pup. That Frill Dog came up on bench and bit Nose-Doll on nose. 'Was Scrap Blue Dollie came. 'Was plenty Scraps! NoseDoll put string round Blue Dollie and threw out over sleepy-bench and singed loud. 'Was finish. Dirty Man came out from under box, and showed his inside-hat to Smalls. They wented all away. He said: 'Garn! You spend fortuns on the movies, you do, but when it comes-to-drammer, you run-like-ares.' He whistle-squeaked and picked up Box and wented.

Time whiles after that, he came again. Smallest said James, which was up-with-the-washing 'Take them down to see near-to.' We wented on- lead, and sat in front-row. Frill Dog, which was called Toby Dog, did all those dash-parlour-tricks for Smalls again. We was ashamed, because he were same-like-us. We said. Toby Dog said back: 'If I weren't on-me-job, I'd give you something to sing for.'...James took away quick. Toby Dog said: 'Night-night! Don't choke yourselves, lovies!'

Time whiles more, Dirty Man came again. Smallest could not go down because of throat. James went and talked him plenty. Man said it were high-class-show-for-crowned-edds, but he would wash-hisself-first. James told Missus. So, Dirty Man came up to Flat, and 'was highclass- show for Smallest and all-us and our Adar. But Toby Dog were slow and sorrowful. Dirty Man said Missus, it were like-master-like-man, because Toby Dog wore-hisself-out-giving-too-much-for-money, and he wanted rest-and-good-kind-home. That whiles, Toby Dog lay on back and rolled eyes like sick-pup. Adar said: 'If those three get together, they will fight till dawn-o-day! Look at Slippers's face!' Missus said did-not-know-quite-what-Master-will-say. James said he could keep in garage at home, so he could-not-come-into-contracts with any one. So, 'was done, and Toby Dog was took down with James to be made well-dog. Three-four day-times after, we'wented down in dog-box-train. Nice Guard-People said Adar we was fit-for-show-as-we-stood.

When we was home, we rabbited round borders for bones, which we had hid-in case of hungries. They was took-all! Slippers said: 'it are that dash-Toby-Dog! C'm with, and house-train him!' We winded him in Wall Garden. We said loud. He did not say. He made his eyes ringy- white round edges. He putted his head under his front. He lifted up behind. He rolled behind-ends-over-heads. He rolled at us! First 'was whitey-eyes: then backends rolling at! We had never seen like that. It were vile undogful! But we did not run. When he rolled quite close, we went back. When he made singings like sick dog, we went back more quick to Own Gods on lawn. Master said me: 'Hullo, Boots! You look as if something had ruffled your self-esteem. What's the fuss?' I did not say. I helped him smoke-pipe like I always do. Harry-with-Spade came and said 'was rabbit in vegetable-gardens. Master got two-bang-gun and went. We heeled quick. Toby Dog came out of garage, full-of-his-dash- self. He said: 'What is?' Slippers said: 'Come and see.' Slippers went into cabbages, and bolted rabbit, which are his 'complishment. Master fired over me and killed. Toby Dog went away like-smoke. Master sent me to back-door with rabbit to give our Adar, which are one of my 'complishments. We went-find Toby Dog. He were on turn in boot-box where James keeps shiney-feet-things. He said: 'What was? What was?' We said: 'Two-bang business.' He said: 'I cannot do! I am afraid! I can not do!' Slippers said: 'You are one dash-common-coward-thief- skug-dog! Where are bones?' Toby Dog told. We digged up and took which was left to old Labrador Kennel for safeness. We told Ravager. He were pleased of seeing us back. Toby Dog came round corner. He said: 'I may be skug-dog, but I am not fool. Let me in on your game, and I will let you in on mine.' Ravager said: 'What are your dirty game?' He said: 'Rats.' And he said he held rat-records at three pubz....aid: 'What are pubz?' He said: 'Lummy! You make me ache!' And he said pubz were where E went after is job. Slippers said: 'What are E?' Toby Dog said: 'Im-which-is-Own-God.' I said: 'What are job?' He said: 'What gets you your grub.' I said: 'That are our Adar when bell goes for Own Gods' Middle Eats, which are Lunch.' He said: 'You know fat lots, you do!' Ravager said: 'No scrappin'! Real-rat to Toby Dog. Job is same as business. After business is trough and sleepy-bench everywhere.' Slippers said: 'His business is dash-parlour-tricks.' And he said about Dirty Man and high-class-show. But he did not say about that in Wall Garden, which we had seen, because we was ashamed. Ravager said: 'Do parlour-tricks!' Toby Dog walked with behind-legs long whiles. He said there was not six-dogs-in-the-perfession like him. He said about rat-records which he held, which E, which were Own God, made betz-on. And he said how James had taken him over to Walk when he came down, and Mister-Kent-Peoples brought plenty-rats to try-out. And he killed eight in half a minute on barn-floor. He said James and Mister-Kent was dretful pleased, and was going-to-skin-the-village-alive as soon as odds-was-right. We did not understand.

Slippers said: 'If you are all this dash-fine-dog, why did Im push you off on James and Missus?' Toby Dog said: 'It is end of London-season for Im. E don't need me awhile. So I play sick-dog and E sells me to nice-kind-people for good-ome. Presently, E will come along and make whistle-squeak. I will hear and go back to me job. P'raps it will be Frill Box and Dollies. P'raps it will be leading blind-man across Marble Arch.' Ravager said: 'Is E blind?' Toby Dog said: 'Blind-enough to get pennies-in-my-cup.' Ravager said: 'I am as near blind-as-makes- no-odds. I am sorry of E.' I told how Ravager had been blinded by nicekind-hen-killer-ladies. Toby Dog said: 'If I had been along 'twould not have happened.' I were dretful angry. Ravager said: 'Drop it, Stoopid! Go and eat grass.'

So 'was walk-about in back-gardens. Presently whiles, James brought cage of rats. And tipped out. I killed one. Slippers one. Toby Dog killed four which ran all different ways. James made-much-of, and said they would peel-thebreeches-off-the-village. Toby Dog were full-of- hisself. Slippers said: ''Ware two-bang-gun! Rabbit it, tripe-hound!' 'Was big say-and-say. Ravager came up from kennel. He said: 'What is silly-row now?' We told. Ravager sat and said: 'I do not like two- bang-guns, and my mother Regan did not. Toby Dog is not tripe-hound. He cannot help himself. It's same as you with swimming.' I said: 'We have long hairs and low-clearance, James says. Of course we do not like water.' Ravager said: ''Same with Toby Dog.' He told us off plenty for rudenesses, and went for sleep-in-fern near The Kennels in Park. Toby Dog said after: 'That is one proper-sort! That is real- true-dog-gent which I will not ever forget!'

'Was bell from house, which our Adar rings for us to help Smallest ride with Moore and Taffy. We rabbited. Toby Dog said: 'I come with.'

It were first ride after Flat-in-Town. 'Was bit-of-a-circus with Taffy because, Moore said, that bone-idle-stable-boy had not exercised enough. But Smallest's legs was grown, and Taffy got-no-change. Smallest were a bit full-of-hisself. Moore said back: 'Don't be too proud, Master Digby! Seats-and-hands is Heaven's gifts.' Smallest were dretful 'shamed, because he is Champion Reserve Smallest. Moore said: 'Not but what you've good-right-to.' Ravager picked all us up in fern near The Kennels. Moore said 'Ravager has been ailing ever since that motor hit him. I don't like it.' Ravager whimpered-to-name. Smallest said: 'Hush! He knows.' Moore said: 'There's not much he don't know.' And he said Ravager had took to lying-out-in-the-fern after Smallest went to Flat, so he could hear Hounds sing on Benches at morning-times for old-sake's-sake. Smallest said: 'Has Uncle Billy found out yet about Upstart?' Moore said: 'I told you too-much-for-your-age after our Lame Fox run. I 'ope you don't carry tales betwixt me and 'is Lordship.' Smallest said: 'Catch me! But I cannot ever be proper Master Fox-hounds 'less you tell me all what you know?' Moore redded over front-of-face. He said: 'Thank you, Master Digby. When your time comes you'll 'ave to deal with such as Upstart. He has the looks-of-a- Nangel and the guts-of-a-mongrel.' And Moore said Rosemary did Upstart's work for him, which was great-grand-daughter of Regan, and ran near-as-mute-as-the-old-lady. And he had watched Upstart at fault time and again, and Rosemary whimpering-in-his-ear to tip-him-the- office, and he taking-all-the-credit. And if, for-any-reason, she was not out, his second-string was Loiterer, which was a soft tail-hound, but with wonderful-tender-nose. And he had watched Upstart at a check play thorn-in-foot till Loiterer came up and put-him-wise. But he said, 'is Lordship was set on Upstart going to Peterborough, which are where Hounds go for Crampion Reserves, and the pity was his looks-and-manners-made-it-a-cert. He said Upstart was born impostor, same as Usurper his sire, which-should-never-'ave-been, but 'is Lordship was misled by his looks, and would not-listen-to-advice. And he said Umbrage-his-Ma were a real-narsty-one on her-side-of-things. He said plenty-more-lots which I forgot. After pull-up, he said: 'Now, Master Digby, you have known the Hounds since you fell into the meal-bin in your petticoats. What do you think?' Smallest said: 'I could hunt any country in all the world with you and three couple which I were let choose. And, if Ravager were well-dog, I would make Uncle Billy present of the odd-couple.' Moore redded all fresh over face. He said: 'Lord love you! I shall be pushing-up-the-daisies long before that! But you 'ave it in you. You 'ave all three in you—Hound, Fox, and Horse! But, to get those three couple four-days-a-week, we have to put up with trash-like-Upstart.'

After whiles, 'was gallop. Slippers and Ravager went with. Toby Dog said me, sitting: 'That were rummy rat that man showed about that dash-clever dog. Tell again.' So I told about Upstart which I do not like, and how he got Musketeer help him fight Egoist for Ravager's place on sleepy-bench that night which Ravager did not cast up. And choked Musketeer after. And were glutton at the break-up-and-eat, which are not proper-game for lead-hounds, Ravager says, and did never go-in-for. Toby Dog said: 'It is cruel-ard on perfessional dog to be knocked out of his job for no fault of hisn, like that real-old-dog- gent of yours.' I said: 'You are not half-bad-dog.' He said: 'I am perfessional. I do not tell all I can do, but I will put you up to proper rattings.' So we wented to Walk and ricked round ricks. He showed how to chop rats-one-chop-one-rat, and not ever to shake, because it loses-time-on-the-count, he said. He told about rat-match at pub-in-village, where he were backed against Fuss, Third Hunt Terrier, which he said were pretty lady-dog which he could give ten rats in the minute and scratch-hisself-at-same-time.

Then we wented back to Labrador Kennel. Ravager was home and told us off proper for shirking-gallop. Slippers came too, because Smallest were at lesson. He said me he were pleased of Toby Dog not keeping with Smallest, because he did not want Smallest to care for. I said: 'That Toby Dog does not want Smallest. He is dash-clever dog which does not do more ever than kill his rat. Leave alone!'

So 'was done. Toby Dog keeped with James about rats 'cept when he went rides with Smallest and us. One time Moore made that bone-idle-stable- boy lay drag to teach Taffy jumps and ditches for cubbing-times. It were dust-bin-herring-tails which I knew. Ravager said drags was stink-pot-stuff and wented home. (Me with.) So Toby Dog led. Time after that time, Smallest took him on lawn and said: 'Do tricks!' Toby Dog sat and scratched ears. Smallest smacked head and said: 'You are impostor like Upstart!' Toby Dog said us after: 'Catch me working overtime for any one 'cept Im and your real-true-dog-gent!' He speaked plenty to Ravager about hunting and hounds and all those things because he said he were perfessional and wanted to know about Ravager's perfession. Ravager liked, and told plenty back. And Toby Dog showed me real rattings and the watch-two-while-you-kill-one game. I sat out in fern with Ravager, which were my true friend since we was almost pups. And Smallest made

Taffy jump-like-fleas, Moore said. So we was all happy dogs, that times.

Then 'was rat-match in village. Toby Dog said it were a cert, but he would give Fuss a look-in for looks' sake. That were night before Bell-Day, and strong Shiny Plate. Slippers and me did walk-abouts in gardens waiting-for-result. (We are not tied up ever now since, that man came over garden-wall to see about the broccoli and were nipped on behinds going-back-over.) Toby Dog came home after match, which he had winned by what-you-dash-like. He said he had winded Dirty Man outside Spotted-Hound-pub in village. We said: 'What rat do you run now?' He said: 'E will need all day to sleep-it-off. E will come to-morrow night. I am glad, because E is Own God. But I am sorry, because you two and your true-old-gent-dog have done me well, and I ad-oped to pay all 'fore I sloped. But E is Own God. When E comes, I go with.' We said: 'Sorry too.' We all went walk-abouts ('was hedgehogs) and sat.

Next day-time was Bell-Day and no-silly-weekend-visitors, Smallest said. We wented all for Middle Eats to Big House, where Proper Man lives, which are called Uncle Billy. Only 'cepting Ravager, which lay out in fern by the Kennels like always. Toby Dog had went to help James collect-debtz-out-of-that-dash-swindling-stable-boy about rat-match. So we did not see.

At Middle Eats was Master-Missus and Smallest and Proper Man and Proper Missus and my friend Butler, which I like, and a new Peoples which was called Jem, which was Master of some Hounds from some-place- else. 'Was plenty Own Gods' say-and-say about hounds-and-feet and those things. Smallest did not say, like he does not ever about Hounds. ('Cept to Moore.)

After coffee-sugar, my friend Butler asked me into laundry-yard to help about rat-in-ivy. I chopped. ('Was cheese.) Butler made carrot-basket for all-Peoples to give Tall Horses. So, 'was walk-to-Kennels, which is always Bell-Day-rat after Middle Eats. I picked up Ravager in fern. He said: 'Run along with. I never go. I am no Hound any more.' I wented into yard with all-Peoples.

'Was Moore which called out Hounds by ones to stand for biscuit. 'Was plenty more say-and-say about legs-and-feet. Smallest did not say, but all hounds speaked him small and soft on flags. That Master Jem said: 'Why, Diggy-boy, they seem to know you as well as Moore!' Smallest said back: 'How vewy odd!' because he does not like old Nursey-Thick- names casting-up. (Same as me when my Adar says 'Bootles.') Missus said small: 'Digby! Behave!' Moore called out Upstart quick, and so 'was loud say-and-say about looks and manners and Belvoir-tans. (We played fleas-on-tum.)

Then Proper Missus put hand-before-front-teeth. So, all-Peoples went to see Tall Horses, 'cept Smallest and Moore. Then Toby Dog came round corner from Tall Horse Kennels, all small and dusty-looking. He said us, out of side-mouth: 'Lummy, what a swine! If he don't scare, I'm a goner. Head my rat!' He made his eyes ringy-white all round, like in Wall Garden. He putted down his head under, and hunched up all his behinds, and rolled himself that undogful way which we had seen. But worse! It were horrabel! Upstart uphackled. But we headed Toby Dog's rat. We singed: 'What is? Oh, we are afraid!' Toby Dog made screamy- draggly noise like cat-pups. And rolled at! Upstart bolted out of yard same as pup-for-cutty-whip, and bolted into fern where Ravager were. We heard plenty yowl-and-kai-yai. Toby Dog unringed his eyes, and was little cheap skug-dog, which walked away. All-Peoples at Horse Kennels came back and said loud about what-on-earth-was-the-matterof-Upstart. Moore said seemingly-he-had-took-offence-at-the-terrier's-doings, and went-off-like-fire-works. That Master Jem said it were dretful- catching-fits, which play-deuce-and-all-with-Packs. Proper Man were angry. Smallest said: 'Won't he be all right for Peterborough, Uncle Billy?' Proper Man said: 'Dash Peterborough! Dash jackal! Never trust Usurper-blood, Moore! I warned you at the time.' Soon whiles, Upstart came back singing snuff-and-butter, Moore said. Moore did not like, and turned him into Kennels which did not like, because he were beaten-hound and telling-it. 'Was big Bench-scrap! Moore went in and rated proper. Smallest looked through window, where Ravager had looked when he came blinded. He said: 'Hooray! Musketeer has took Upstart's place and Upstart has Loiterer's—right at edge by door!'

Soon whiles, all-Peoples went back to tea saying say-and-say about fits. Smallest walked behind with Slippers and me. Time whiles he danced. We helped. We picked up Ravager in fern. I said: 'We heard. Did you get?' Ravager said: 'I could not help. He fell over me like blind dog. I got him across the loins and wrenched him on his back. But he was in a hurry. What began it?' I told all what Toby Dog had done to Upstart. Ravager said: 'That is a dash-odd-little-dog, but I like him. He hunts with his head. ''What was the Bench-row about afterwards?' I told how Upstart had lost benchplace to Musketeer and had been gived Loiterer's. Ravager said: 'Good rat to Toby Dog! That place was colder than Cotswold when I was a young 'un. Now I am happy!' We wented all in, and plenty things under tea-table. Ravager did not take. He sat by Proper Man, head-on-knee. Proper Man said: 'What's brought you back to your old 'legiance, old fellow? You belong to Digby now.' Ravager said soft and kissed hand. Proper Man said: ''Queer as his Mother before him!' After lots more say-and-say we all wented home 'cross Park. Smallest danced and singed loud till kennel- up. We went upstairs to help, like always when Guvvy lets. Ravager came with. That dash-Guvvy said him rudenesses on the stairs. Adar said her: 'Beg pardon, Miss, but no one ever questions the old gentleman's comings-and-goings in this house.' Ravager tail-thumped and kissed Smallest's two hands at pyjarm-time. He went down stairs slow, because he never-comes-up-to-the-top-landing. He said me: 'Now I am all-round-happy-hound. Come see me later, Stoopid. I've something to tell you.' I helped Master-Missus spend-happy-evening, like I do, till Adar came to take out and give night-bones.

After, I went for walk-abouts with Slippers, because Shiny Plate were shiny-strong. James came and called Toby Dog, which he could not find. And dashed and wented. Toby Dog came out behind rhubarb-pots. He asked about Upstart. We told. He were happy dog. He said he had near-given- Alsatians-fits-that-way. He asked if old true-gent-dog Ravager were pleased of his doings. He said he could not go-see him, because he were on-dooty expecting Im which was Own God any minute now. And he said he were plenty skug-cur about that two-bang business which were not perfessional. We said he were wonderful brave dog about Upstart, which me and Slippers would not have taken on. He said: 'Fairy Ann! Fairy Ann!' But he were most-happy dog. Presently whiles 'was whistle- squeak down lane by Orchard. Toby Dog said: 'That's Im. S'long!' He wented all little through hedge. Dirty Man said outside: 'Oh! You've come, 'ave yer? Come orn!'

Please, that is finish all about Toby Dog, which Ravager liked. (Me too.)

Slippers went-to-bone. I wented Labrador Kennel to speak Ravager, and opied door with my nose like I can.

Ravager said: 'Who is?' I said: 'Boots.' He said: 'I know that, but Who Else came in with?' I said: 'Only Boots.' He said 'There is Some- one-else-more! Look!' I said 'Toby Dog has gone back to Im. Slippers has kennelled-up. It is only me-by-selfs. But I am looking.' 'Was only Ravager and me everywhere. Ravager said: 'Sorry! I am getting blinder every day. Come and sit close, Stoopid.' I jumped on sleepy-bench, like always, night-times. He said: 'Sit closer. I am cold. Curl in between paws, so I can lay head-onback.' So 'was.

Presently whiles, he said: 'If this black frost holds, good-bye hunting.' I said: 'It is warm leaves-on night, with Shiny plate and rabbits-in-grass.' He said: 'I'll take your word for it,' and put head on my back, long whiles all still. Then he said: 'I know now what it was I meant to tell you, Stoopid. Never wrench a hound as heavy as yourself at my time of life. It plays the dickens with your head and neck.' And he hickied. I said: 'Sick-up, and be comfy.' He said: 'It is not tum-hickey. It is in throat and neck. Lie a bit closer.' He dropped head and sleeped. Me too. Presently whiles, he said: 'Give me my place on the Bench or I'll have the throat out of you!' I said: 'Here is all own bench and all own place.' He said: 'Sorry! I were with the old lot.' Then he dropped head-on-me and sleep-hunted with hounds which he knew when he came up from Walk. I heard and I were afraid. I hunched-up-back to wake him. He said, all small, 'Don't go away! I am old blind hound! I am afraid! I am afraid of kennel-that-moves! I cannot see where here is!' I said: 'Here is Boots.' He said: 'Sorry! You are always true friend of Ravager. Keep close, in case if I bump.' He sleeped more, and Shiny Plate went on across over. Then he said: 'I can see! 'Member Bucket on my head? 'Member Cow-pups we was whacked for chasing-pounds-off? 'Member Bull-in-Park? I can see all those things, Stoopid. I am happy-hound! Sorry if I were a noosance!'

So he sleeped long whiles. Me too, next to chest between paws. When I unsleeped, Shiny Plate was going-to-ground, and hen-gents was saying at Walk, and fern-in-Park was all shiny. Ravager unsleeped slow. He yawned. He said, small: 'Here is one happy hound, with 'nother happy day ahead!' He shaked himself and sat up. He said loud: 'It is morning! Sing, all you Sons of Benches! Sing!' Then he fell down all- one-piece, and did not say. I lay still because I were afraid, because he did not say any more. Presently whiles, Slippers came quiet. He said: 'I have winded Something which makes me afraid. What is?' I said: 'It is Ravager which does not say any more. I am afraid, too.' He said: 'I are sorry, but Ravager is big strong dog. He will be all right soon.' He wented away and sat under Smallest's window, in case of Smallest singing-out at getting-up-time, like he always does. I waited till my Adar opened kitchen-curtains for brekker. I called. She came quick. She said: 'Oh, my Bootles! Me poor little Bootles!' Ravager did not say her anything. She wented away to tell. I sat with, in case if he might unsleep. Soonwhiles, all-Peoples came—Smallest, Master-Missus, and Harry-with-Spade. Slippers too, which stayed by his Smallest and kissed hands to make him happy-pup. They took up to Orchard. Harry digged and put under like bone. But it were my Ravager. Smallest said dretful loud, and they wented away—all—all—'cept my Adar which sat on wheel-barrow and hickied. I tried to undig. She picked up, and carried to kitchen, and held me tight with apron over heads and hickied loud. They would not let me undig more. There was tie-up. After what whiles, I went for walk-abouts, in case if p'raps I could find him. I wented to his lie-down in fern. I wented to Walk and Wood Ride and Micefield, and all those old places which was. He were not there. So I came back and waited in Orchard, where he cast up blinded that night, which were my true friend Ravager, which were always good to me since we was almost pups, and never minded of my short legs or because I were stoopid. But he did not come...

Please, this is finish for always about Ravager and me and all those times.

Please, I am very little small mis'able dog!...I do not understand!...I do not understand!

THE SUPPLICATION OF THE BLACK ABERDEEN

I PRAY! My little body and whole span
Of years is Thine, my Owner and my Man.
For Thou hast made me—unto Thee I owe
This dim, distressed half-soul that hurts me so,
Compact of every crime, but, none the less,
Broken by knowledge of its naughtiness.
Put me not from Thy Life—'tis all I know.
If Thou forsake me, whither shall I go?

Thine is the Voice with which my Day begins:
Thy Foot my refuge, even in my sins.
Thine Honour hurls me forth to testify
Against the Unclean and Wicked passing by.
(But when Thou callest they are of Thy Friends,
Who readier than I to make amends?)
I was Thy Deputy with high and low—
If Thou dismiss me, whither shall I go?

I have been driven forth on gross offence
That took no reckoning of my penitence,
And, in my desolation—faithless me!—
Have crept for comfort to a woman's knee!
Now I return, self-drawn, to meet the just
Reward of Riot, Theft and Breach of Trust.
Put me not from Thy Life—though this is so.
If Thou forsake me, whither shall I go?

Into The Presence, flattening while I crawl—
From head to tail, I do confess it all.
Mine was the fault—deal me the stripes—but spare
The Pointed Finger which I cannot bear!
The Dreadful Tone in which my Name is named,
That sends me 'neath the sofa-frill ashamed!
(Yet, to be near Thee, I would face that woe.)
If Thou reject me, whither shall I go?

Thy Servant a Dog

Can a gift turn Thee? I will bring mine all—
My Secret Bone, my Throwing-Stick, my Ball.
Or wouldst Thou sport? Then watch me hunt awhile,
Chasing, not after conies, but Thy Smile,
Content, as breathless on the turf I sit,
Thou shouldst deride my little legs and wit—
Ah! Keep me in Thy Life for a fool's show!
If Thou deny me, whither shall I go!...

Is the Dark gone? The Light of Eyes restored?
The Countenance turned meward, O my Lord?
The Paw accepted, and—for all to see—
The Abject Sinner throned upon the Knee?
The Ears bewrung, and Muzzle scratched because
He is forgiven, and All is as It was?
Now am I in Thy Life, and since 'tis so—
That Cat awaits the Judgment. May I go?

A SEA DOG

WHEN that sloop known to have been in the West Indies trade for a century had been repaired by Mr. Randolph of Stephano's Island, there arose between him and her owner, Mr. Gladstone Gallop, a deep-draught pilot, Admiral (retired) Lord Heatleigh, and Mr. Winter Vergil, R.N. (also retired), the question how she would best sail. This could only be settled on trial trips of the above Committee, ably assisted by Lil, Mr. Randolph's mongrel fox-terrier, and, sometimes, the Commander of the H.M.S. Bulleana, who was the Admiral's nephew.

Lil had been slid into a locker to keep dry till they reached easier water. The others lay aft watching the breadths of the all-coloured seas. Mr. Gallop at the tiller, which had replaced the wheel, said as little as possible, but condescended, before that company, to make his boat show off among the reefs and passages of coral where his business and delight lay.

Mr. Vergil, not for the first time, justified himself to the Commander for his handling of the great Parrot Problem, which has been told elsewhere. The Commander tactfully agreed with the main principle that—man, beast, or bird—discipline must be preserved in the Service; and that, so far, Mr. Vergil had done right in disrating, by cutting off her tail-feathers, Josephine, alias Jemmy Reader, the West African parrot...

He himself had known a dog—his own dog, in fact—almost born, and altogether brought up, in a destroyer, who had not only been rated and disrated, but also re-rated and promoted, completely understanding the while what had happened, and why.

'Come out and listen,' said Mr. Randolph, reaching into the locker. 'This'll do you good.' Lil came out, limp over his hand, and braced herself against the snap and jerk of a sudden rip which Mr. Gallop was cutting across. He had stood in to show the Admiral Gallop's Island whose original grantees had freed their Carib slaves more than a hundred years ago. These had naturally taken their owners' family name; so that now there were many Gallops—gentle, straight-haired men of substance and ancestry, with manners to match, and instinct, beyond all knowledge, of their home waters—from Panama, that is, to Pernambuco.

The Commander told a tale of an ancient destroyer on the China station which, with three others of equal seniority, had been hurried over to the East Coast of England when the Navy called up her veterans for the War. How Malachi—Michael, Mike, or Mickey—throve aboard the old Makee-do, on whose books he was rated as 'Pup,' and learned to climb oily steel ladders by hooking his fore-feet over the rungs. How he was used as a tippet round his master's neck on the bridge of cold nights. How he had his own special area, on deck by the raft, sacred to his private concerns, and never did anything one hair's-breadth outside it. How he possessed an officers' steward of the name of Furze, his devoted champion and trumpeter through the little flotilla which worked together on convoy and escort duties in the North Sea. Then the wastage of war began to tell and...The Commander turned to the Admiral.

'They dished me out a new Volunteer sub for First Lieutenant—a youngster of nineteen—with a hand on him like a ham and a voice like a pneumatic riveter, though he couldn't pronounce "r" to save himself. I found him sitting on the wardroom table with his cap on, scratching his leg. He said to me, "Well, old top, and what's the big idea for to-mowwow's agony?" I told him—and a bit more. He wasn't upset. He was really grateful for a hint how things were run on "big ships" as he called 'em. (Makee-do was three hundred ton, I think.) He'd served in Coastal Motor Boats retrieving corpses off the Cornish coast. He told me his skipper was a vet who called the swells "fuwwows" and thought he ought to keep between 'em. His name was Eustace Cyril Chidden; and his papa was a sugar-refiner...'

Surprise was here expressed in various quarters; Mr. Winter Vergil adding a few remarks on the decadence of the New Navy.

'No,' said the Commander. 'The "old top" business had nothing to do with it. He just didn't know—that was all. But Mike took to him at once.

'Well, we were booted out, one night later, on special duty. No marks or lights of course—raining, and confused seas. As soon as I'd made an offing, I ordered him to take the bridge. Cyril trots up, his boots greased, the complete N.O. Mike and I stood by in the chart-room. Pretty soon, he told off old Shide, our Torpedo Coxswain, for being a quarter-point off his course. (He was, too; but he wasn't pleased.) A bit later, Cyril ships his steam-riveter voice and tells him he's all over the card, and if he does it again he'll be "welieved." It went on like this the whole trick; Michael and me waiting for Shide to mutiny. When Shide came off, I asked him what he thought we'd drawn. "Either a dud or a diamond," says Shide. "There's no middle way with that muster." That gave me the notion that Cyril might be worth kicking. So we all had a hack at him. He liked it. He did, indeed! He said it was so "intewesting" because Makee-do "steered like a witch," and no one ever dreamed of trying to steer C.M.B.'s. They must have been bloody pirates in that trade, too. He was used to knocking men about to make 'em attend. He threatened a stay-maker's apprentice (they were pushing all sorts of shore-muckings at us) for imitating his lisp. It was smoothed over, but the man made the most of it. He was a Bolshie before we knew what to call 'em. He kicked Michael once when he thought no one was looking, but Furze saw, and the blighter got his head cut on a hatch-coaming. That didn't make him any sweeter.'

A twenty-thousand-ton liner, full of thirsty passengers, passed them on the horizon. Mr. Gallop gave her name and that of the pilot in charge, with some scandal as to her weakness at certain speeds and turns.

'Not so good a sea-boat as her!' He pointed at a square-faced tug—or but little larger—punching dazzle-white wedges out of indigo-blue.

The Admiral stood up and pronounced her a North Sea mine-sweeper.

''Was. 'Ferry-boat now,' said Mr. Gallop. ''Never been stopped by weather since ten years.'

The Commander shuddered aloud, as the old thing shovelled her way along. 'But she sleeps dry,' he said. 'We lived in a foot of water. Our decks leaked like anything. We had to shore our bulkheads with broomsticks practically every other trip. Most of our people weren't broke to the life, and it made 'em sticky. I had to tighten things up.'

The Admiral and Mr. Vergil nodded.

'Then, one day, Chidden came to me and said there was some feeling on the lower deck because Mike was still rated as "Pup" after all his sea-time. He thought our people would like him being promoted to Dog. I asked who'd given 'em the notion. "Me," says Cyril. "I think it'll help de-louse 'em mowally." Of course I instructed him to go to Hell and mind his own job. Then I notified that Mike was to be borne on the ship's books as Able Dog Malachi. I was on the bridge when the watches were told of it. They cheered. Fo'c'sle afloat; galley-fire missing as usual; but they cheered. That's the Lower Deck.'

Mr. Vergil rubbed hands in assent.

'Did Mike know, Mr. Randolph? He did. He used to sniff forrard to see what the men's dinners were going to be. If he approved, he went and patronised 'em. If he didn't, he came to the wardroom for sharks and Worcester sauce. He was a great free-fooder. But—the day he was promoted Dog—he trotted round all messes and threw his little weight about like an Admiral's inspection—Uncle. (He wasn't larger than Lil, there.) Next time we were in for boiler-clean, I got him a brass collar engraved with his name and rating. I swear it was the only bit of bright work in the North Sea all the War. They fought to polish it. Oh, Malachi was a great Able Dog, those days, but he never forgot his decencies...'

Mr. Randolph here drew Lil's attention to this.

'Well, and then our Bolshie-bird oozed about saying that a ship where men were treated like dogs and vice versa was no catch. Quite true, if correct; but it spreads despondency and attracts the baser elements. You see?'

'Anything's an excuse when they are hanging in the wind,' said Mr. Vergil. 'And what might you have had for the standing-part of your tackle?'

'You know as well as I do, Vergil. The old crowd—Gunner, Chief Engineer, Cook, Chief Stoker, and Torpedo Cox. But, no denyin', we were hellish uncomfy. Those old thirty-knotters had no bows or freeboard to speak of, and no officers' quarters. (Sleep with your Gunner's socks in your mouth, and so on.) You remember 'em, sir?' The Admiral did—when the century was young—and some pirate-hunting behind muddy islands. Mr. Gallop drank it in. His war experiences had ranged no further than the Falklands, which he had visited as one of the prize-crew of a German sailing-ship picked up Patagonia-way and sent south under charge of a modern sub-lieutenant who had not the haziest notion how to get the canvas off a barque in full career for vertical cliffs. He told the tale. Mr. Randolph, who had heard it before, brought out a meal sent by Mrs. Vergil. Mr. Gallop laid the sloop on a slant where she could look after herself while they ate. Lil earned her share by showing off her few small tricks.

'Mongrels are always smartest,' said Mr. Randolph half defiantly.

'Don't call 'em mongrels.' The Commander tweaked Lil's impudent little ear. 'Mike was a bit that way. Call 'em "mixed." There's a difference.'

The tiger-lily flush inherited from his ancestors on the mainland flared a little through the brown of Mr. Gallop's cheek. 'Right,' said he. 'There's a heap differ 'twixt mongrel and mixed.'

And in due time, so far as Time was on those beryl floors, they came back to the Commander's tale.

It covered increasing discomforts and disgusts, varied by escapes from being blown out of water by their own side in fog; affairs with submarines; arguments with pig-headed convoy-captains, and endless toil to maintain Makee-do abreast of her work which the growing ignorance and lowering morale of the new drafts made harder.

'The only one of us who kept his tail up was Able Dog Malachi. He was an asset, let alone being my tippet on watch. I used to button his front and hind legs into my coat, with two turns of my comforter over all. Did he like it? He had to. It was his station in action. But he had his enemies. I've told you what a refined person he was. Well, one day, a buzz went round that he had defiled His Majesty's quarterdeck. Furze reported it to me, and, as he said, "Beggin' your pardon, it might as well have been any of us, sir, as him." I asked the little fellow what he had to say for himself; confronting him with the circumstantial evidence of course. He was very offended. I knew it by the way he stiffened next time I took him for tippet. Chidden was sure there had been some dirty work somewhere; but he thought a Court of Inquiry might do good and settle one or two other things that were loose in the ship. One party wanted Mike disrated on the evidence. They were the—'

'I know 'em,' sighed Mr. Vergil; his eyes piercing the years behind him. 'The other lot wanted to find out the man who had tampered with the—the circumstantial evidence and pitch him into the ditch. At that particular time, we were escorting mine-sweepers—every one a bit jumpy. I saw what Chidden was driving at, but I wasn't sure our crowd here were mariners enough to take the inquiry seriously. Chidden swore they were. He'd been through the Crystal Palace training himself. Then I said, "Make it so. I waive my rights as the dog's owner. Discipline's discipline, tell 'em; and it may be a counter-irritant."

'The trouble was there had been a fog, on the morning of the crime, that you couldn't spit through; so no one had seen anything. Naturally, Mike sculled about as he pleased; but his regular routine— he slept with me and Chidden in the wardroom—was to take off from our stomachs about three bells in the morning watch (half-past five) and trot up topside to attend to himself in his own place. But the evidence, you see, was found near the bandstand—the after six- pounder; and accused was incapable of testifying on his own behalf... Well, that Court of Inquiry had it up and down and thort-ships all the time we were covering the minesweepers. It was a foul area; rather too close to Fritz's coast. We only drew seven feet, so we were more or less safe. Our supporting cruisers lay on the edge of the area. Fritz had messed that up months before, and lots of his warts—mines— had broke loose and were bobbing about; and then our specialists had swept it, and laid down areas of their own, and so on. Any other time all hands would have been looking out for loose mines. (They have horns that nod at you in a sickly-friendly-frisky way when they roll.) But, while Mike's inquiry was on, all hands were too worked-up over it to spare an eye outboard...Oh, Mike knew, Mr. Randolph. Make no mistake. He knew he was in for trouble. The Prosecution were too crafty for him. They stuck to the evidence—the locus in quo and so on...Sentence? Disrating to Pup again, which carried loss of badge- of-rank—his collar. Furze took it off, and Mickey licked his hand and Furze wept like Peter...Then Mickey hoicked himself up to the bridge to tell me about it, and I made much of him. He was a distressed little dog. You know how they snuffle and snuggle up when they feel hurt.'

Though the question was to Mr. Randolph, all hands answered it.

'Then our people went to dinner with this crime on their consciences. Those who felt that way had got in on me through Michael.'

'Why did you make 'em the chance?' the Admiral demanded keenly.

'To divide the sheep from the goats, sir. It was time...Well, we were second in the line—How-come and Fan-kwai next astern and Hop-hell, our flagship, leading. Withers was our Senior Officer. We called him "Joss" because he was always so infernally lucky. It was flat calm with patches of fog, and our sweepers finished on time. While we were escorting 'em back to our cruisers, Joss picked up some wireless buzz about a submarine spotted from the air, surfacing over to the north- east-probably recharging. He detached How-come and Fan-kwai to go on with our sweepers, while him and me went-look-see. We dodged in and out of fog-patches—two-mile visibility one minute and blind as a bandage the next-then a bit of zincy sun like a photograph—and so on. Well, breaking out of one of these patches we saw a submarine recharging-hatches open, and a man on deck—not a mile off our port quarter. We swung to ram and, as he came broadside on to us, I saw Hop-hell slip a mouldie—fire a torpedo—at him, and my Gunner naturally followed suit. By the mercy o' God, they both streaked ahead and astern him, because the chap on deck began waving an open brolly at us like an old maid hailing a bus. That fetched us up sliding on our tails, as you might say. Then he said, "What do you silly bastards think you're doin'?" (He was Conolly, and some of his crowd had told us, ashore, that the brolly was his private code. That's why we didn't fire on sight, sir.—"Red" Conolly, not "Black.") He told us he'd gone pretty close inshore on spec the night before and had been hunted a bit and had to lie doggo, and he'd heard three or four big ships go over him. He told us where that was, and we stood by till he'd finished recharging and we gave him his position and he sculled off. He said it was hellish thick over towards the coast, but there seemed to be something doing there. So we proceeded, on the tip Conolly gave us...Oh, wait a minute! Joss's Gunner prided himself on carrying all the silhouettes of Fritz's navy in his fat head, and he had sworn that Conolly's craft was the duplicate of some dam U-boat. Hence his shot. I believe Joss pretty well skinned him for it, but that didn't alter the fact we'd only one mouldie apiece left to carry on with...

'Presently Joss fetched a sharp sheer to port, and I saw his bow-wave throw off something that looked like the horns of a mine; but they were only three or four hock bottles. We don't drink hock much at sea.'

Mr. Randolph and Mr. Gallop smiled. There are few liquors that the inhabitants of Stephano's Island do not know—bottled, barrelled, or quite loose.

The Commander continued.

'Then Joss told me to come alongside and hold his hand, because he felt nervous.'

The Commander here explained how, with a proper arrangement of fenders, a trusty Torpedo Cox at the wheel, and not too much roll on, destroyers of certain types can run side by side close enough for their captains to talk even confidentially to each other. He ended, 'We used to slam those old dowagers about like sampans.'

'You youngsters always think you discovered navigation,' said the Admiral. 'Where did you steal your fenders from?'

'That was Chidden's pigeon in port, sir. He was the biggest thief bar three in the Service. C.M.B.'s are a bad school...So, then, we proceeded—bridge to bridge—chinning all comfy. Joss said those hock bottles and the big ships walking over Conolly interested him strangely. It was shoaling and we more or less made out the set of the tide. We didn't chuck anything overboard, though; and just about sunset in a clear patch we passed another covey of hock bottles. Mike spotted them first. He used to poke his little nose up under my chin if he thought I was missing anything. Then it got blind-thick, as Conolly said it would, and there was an ungodly amount of gibber on the wireless. Joss said it sounded like a Fritz tip-and-run raid somewhere and we might come in handy if the fog held. (You couldn't see the deck from the bridge.) He said I'd better hand him over my surviving mouldie because he was going to slip 'em himself hence- forward, and back his own luck. My tubes were nothing to write home about, anyhow. So we passed the thing over, and proceeded. We cut down to bare steerage-way at last (you couldn't see your hand before your face by then) and we listened. You listen better in fog.'

'But it doesn't give you your bearings,' said Mr. Gallop earnestly.

'True. Then you fancy you hear things—like we did. Then Mike began poking up under my chin again. He didn't imagine things. I passed the word to Joss, and a minute or two after, we heard voices—they sounded miles away. Joss said, "That's the hock-bottler. He's hunting his home channel. I hope he's too bothered to worry about us; but if this stuff lifts we'll wish we were Conolly." I buttoned Mike well in to me bosom and took an extra turn of my comforter round him, and those ghastly voices started again—up in the air this time, and all down my neck. Then something big went astern, both screws—then ahead dead slow— then shut off. Joss whispered, "He's atop of us!" I said, "Not yet. Mike's winding .. him to starboard!" The little chap had his head out of my comforter again, sniffin' and poking my chin...And then, by God! the blighter slid up behind us to starboard. We couldn't see him. We felt him take what wind there was, and we smelt him—hot and sour. He was passing soundings to the bridge, by voice. I suppose he thought he was practically at home. Joss whispered, "Go ahead and cuddle him till you hear me yap. Then amuse him. I shall slip my second by the flare of his batteries while he's trying to strafe you." So he faded off to port and I went ahead slow—oh, perishing slow! Shide swore afterwards that he made out the loom of the brute's stern just in time to save his starboard propeller. That was when my heart stopped working. Then I heard my port fenders squeak like wet cork along his side, and there we were cuddling the hock-bottler! If you lie close enough to anything big he can't theoretically depress his guns enough to get you.'

Mr. Gallop smiled again. He had known that game played in miniature by a motor-launch off the Bahamas under the flaring bows of a foreign preventive boat.

'...Funny to lie up against a big ship eaves-dropping that way. We could hear her fans and engine-room bells going, and some poor devil with a deuce of a cough. I don't know how long it lasted, but, all that awful while, Fritz went on with his housekeeping overhead. I'd sent Shide aft to the relieving tackles—I had an idea the wheel might go—and put Chidden on the twelve-pounder on the bridge. My Gunner had the forward six-pounders, and I kept Makee-do cuddling our friend. Then I heard Joss yap once, and then the devil of a clang. He'd got his first shot home. We got in three rounds of the twelve, and the sixes cut into her naked skin at-oh, fifteen feet it must have been. Then we all dived aft. (My ewe-torpedo wouldn't have been any use anyhow. The head would have hit her side before the tail was out of the tube.) She woke up and blazed off all starboard batteries, but she couldn't depress to hit us. The blast of 'em was enough, though. It knocked us deaf and sick and silly. It pushed my bridge and the twelve-pounder over to starboard in a heap, like a set of fire-irons, and it opened up the top of the forward funnel and flared it out like a tulip. She put another salvo over us that winded us again. Mind you, we couldn't hear that! We felt it. Then we were jarred sideways—a sort of cow-kick, and I thought it was finish. Then there was a sort of ripping woolly feel—not a noise—in the air, and I saw the haze of a big gun's flash streaking up overhead at abou' thirty degrees. It occurred to me that she was rolling away from us and it was time to stand clear. So we went astern a bit. And that haze was the only sight I got of her from first to last!...After a while, we felt about to take stock of the trouble. Our bridge-wreckage was listing us a good deal to starboard: the funnel spewed smoke all over the shop and some of the stays were cut; wireless smashed; compasses crazy of course; raft and all loose fittings lifted overboard; hatches and such-like strained or jammed and the deck leaking a shade more than usual. But no casualties. A few ratings cut and bruised by being chucked against things, and, of course, general bleeding from the nose and ears. But— funny thing—we all shook like palsy. That lasted longest. We all went about shouting and shaking. Shock, I suppose.'

'And Mike?' Mr. Randolph asked.

'Oh, he was all right. He had his teeth well into my comforter throughout. 'First thing after action, he hopped down to the wardroom and lapped up pints. Then he tried to dig the gas taste out of his mouth with his paws. Then he wanted to attend to himself, but he found all his private area gone west with the other unsecured gadgets. He was very indignant and told Furze about it. Furze bellows into my ear, "That's proof it couldn't have been him on the quarterdeck, sir, because, if ever any one was justified in being promiscuous, now would be the time. But 'e's as dainty as a duchess."...Laugh away!—It wasn't any laughing matter for Don Miguel.'

'—I beg his pardon! How did you settle his daintiness?' said the Admiral.

'I gave him special leave to be promiscuous, and just because I laughed he growled like a young tiger...You mayn't believe what comes next, but it's fact. Five minutes later, the whole ship was going over Mike's court-martial once again. They were digging out like beavers to repair damage, and chinning at the top of their voices. And a year—no—six months before, half of 'em were Crystal Palace naval exhibits!'

'Same with shanghaied hands,' said Mr. Gallop, putting her about with a nudge of his shoulder on the tiller and some almost imperceptible touch on a sheet. The wind was rising.

'...I ran out of that fog at last like running out of a tunnel. I worked my way off shore, more or less by soundings, till I picked up a star to go home by. Arguin' that Joss 'ud do about the same, I waited for him while we went on cutting away what was left of the bridge and restaying the funnel. It was flat calm still; the coast-fog lying all along like cliffs as far as you could see. 'Dramatic, too, because, when the light came, Joss shot out of the fog three or four miles away and hared down to us clearing his hawsers for a tow. We did look rather a dung-barge. I signalled we were all right and good for thirteen knots, which was one dam lie...Well...so then we proceeded line-ahead, and Joss sat on his depth-charge-rack aft, semaphoring all about it to me on my fo'c'sle-head. He had landed the hock-bottler to port with his first shot. His second—it touched off her forward magazine—was my borrowed one; but he reported it as "a torpedo from the deck of my Second in Command!" She was showing a blaze through the fog then, so it was a sitting shot—at about a hundred yards, he thought. He never saw any more of her than I did, but he smelt a lot of burnt cork. She might have been some old craft packed with cork like a life-boat for a tip-and-run raid. We never knew.'

Even in that short time the wind and the purpose of the waves had strengthened.

'All right,' said Mr. Gallop. 'Nothin' due 'fore to-morrow.' But Mr. Randolph, under sailing-orders from Mrs. Vergil, had the oilskins out ere the sloop lay down to it in earnest. 'Then—after that?' said he.

'Well, then we proceeded; Joss flag-wagging me his news, and all hands busy on our funnel and minor running-repairs, but all arguin' Mike's case hotter than ever. And all of us shaking.'

'Where was Mike?' Mr. Randolph asked as a cut wave-top slashed across the deck.

'Doing tippet for me on the fo'c'sle, and telling me about his great deeds. He never barked, but he could chin like a Peke. Then Joss changed course. I thought it might be mines, but having no bridge I had no command of sight. Then we passed a torpedo-bearded man lolling in a life-belt, with his head on his arms, squinting at us—like a drunk at a pub...Dead? Quite...You never can tell how the lower deck'll take anything. They stared at it and our Cook said it looked saucy. That was all. Then Furze screeched: "But for the grace o' God that might be bloody-all of us!" And he carried on with that bit of the Marriage Service—"I ree-quire an' charge you as ye shall answer at the Day of Judgment, which blinkin' hound of you tampered with the evidence re Malachi. Remember that beggar out in the wet is listenin'." 'Sounds silly, but it gave me the creeps at the time. I heard the Bolshie say that a joke was a joke if took in the right spirit. Then there was a bit of a mix-up round the funnel, but of course I was busy swapping yarns with Joss. When I went aft—I didn't hurry—our Chief Stoker was standing over Furze, while Chidden and Shide were fending off a small crowd who were lusting for the Bolshie's blood. (He had a punch, too, Cywil.) It looked to me—but I couldn't have sworn to it—that the Chief Stoker scraped up a knife with his foot and hoofed it overboard.'

'Knife!' the shocked Admiral interrupted.

'A wardroom knife, sir, with a ground edge on it. Furze had been a Leicester Square waiter or pimp or something, for ten years, and he'd contracted foreign habits. By the time I took care to reach the working-party, they were carrying on like marionettes, because they hadn't got over their shakes, you see...I didn't do anything. I didn't expect the two men Chidden had biffed 'ud complain of him as long as the Bolshie was alive; and our Chief Stoker had mopped up any awkward evidence against Furze. All things considered, I felt rather sorry for the Bolshie...Chidden came to me in the wardroom afterwards, and said the man had asked to be "segwegated" for his own safety. Oh yes!—he'd owned up to tampering with the evidence. I said I couldn't well crime the swine for blackening a dog's character; but I'd reinstate and promote Michael, and the lower deck might draw their own conclusions. "Then they'll kill the Bolshie," says the young 'un. "No," I said, "C.M.B.'s don't know everything, Cywil. They'll put the fear of death on him, but they won't scupper him. What's he doing now?" "Weconstwucting Mike's pwivate awea, with Shide and Furze standing over him gwinding their teeth." "Then he's safe," I said. "I'll send Mike up to see if it suits him. But what about Dawkins and Pratt?" Those were the two men Cyril had laid out while the Chief Stoker was quenching the engine-room ratings. They didn't love the Bolshie either. "Full of beans and blackmail!" he says. "I told 'em I'd saved 'em fwom being hung, but they want a sardine-supper for all hands when we get in."'

'But what's a Chief Stoker doin' on the upper deck?' said Mr. Vergil peevishly, as he humped his back against a solid douche.

'Preserving discipline. Ours could mend anything from the wardroom clock to the stove, and he'd make a sailor of anything on legs—same as you used to, Mr. Vergil...Well, and so we proceeded, and when Chidden reported the "awea" fit for use I sent Mike up to test it.'

'Did Mike know?' said Mr. Randolph.

'Don't ask me what he did or didn't, or you might call me a liar. The Bolshie apologised to Malachi publicly, after Chidden gave out that I'd promoted him to Warrant Dog "for conspicuous gallantwy in action and giving valuable information as to enemy's whaiwabouts in course of same." So Furze put his collar on again, and gave the Bolshie his name and rating.'

The Commander quoted it—self-explanatory indeed, but not such as the meanest in His Majesty's Service would care to answer to even for one day.

'It went through the whole flotilla.' The Commander repeated it, while the others laughed those gross laughs women find so incomprehensible.

'Did he stay on?' said Mr. Vergil. 'Because I knew a stoker in the old Minotaur who cut his throat for half as much as that. It takes 'em funny sometimes.'

'He stayed with us all right; but he experienced a change of heart, Mr. Vergil.'

'I've seen such in my time,' said the Ancient.

The Admiral nodded to himself. Mr. Gallop at the tiller half rose as he peered under the foresail, preparatory to taking a short-cut where the coral gives no more second chance than a tiger's paw. In half an hour they were through that channel. In an hour, they had passed the huge liner tied up and discharging her thirsty passengers opposite the liquor-shops that face the quay. Some, who could not suffer the four and a half minutes' walk to the nearest hotel, had already run in and come out tearing the wrappings off the whisky bottles they had bought. Mr. Gallop held on to the bottom of the harbour and fetched up with a sliding curtsey beneath the mangroves by the boat-shed...

'I don't know whether I've given you quite the right idea about my people,' said the Commander at the end. 'I used to tell 'em they were the foulest collection of sweeps ever forked up on the beach. In some ways they were. But I don't want you to make any mistake. When it came to a pinch they were the salt of the earth—the very salt of God's earth—blast 'em and bless 'em. Not that it matters much now. We've got no Navy.'

HIS APOLOGIES

MASTER, this is Thy Servant. He is rising eight weeks old.
He is mainly Head and Tummy. His legs are uncontrolled.
But Thou hast forgiven his ugliness, and settled him on Thy knee...
Art Thou content with Thy Servant? He is very comfy with Thee.

Master, behold a Sinner? He hath done grievous wrong.
He hath defiled Thy Premises through being kept in too long.
Wherefore his nose has been rubbed in the dirt, and his self-respect has been bruiséd.
Master, pardon Thy Sinner, and see he is properly looséd.

Master—again Thy Sinner! This that was once Thy Shoe,
He hath found and taken and carried aside, as fitting matter to chew.
Now there is neither blacking nor tongue, and the Housemaid has us in tow.
Master, remember Thy Servant is young, and tell her to let him go!

Master, extol Thy Servant! He hath met a most Worthy Foe!
There has been fighting all over the Shop—and into the Shop also!
Till cruel umbrellas parted the strife (or I might have been choking him yet).
But Thy Servant has had the Time of his Life—and now shall we call on the vet?

Master, behold Thy Servant! Strange children came to play,
And because they fought to caress him, Thy Servant wentedst away.
But now that the Little Beasts have gone, he has returned to see
(Brushed—with his Sunday collar on—) what they left over from tea.

* * * * *

Master, pity Thy Servant! He is deaf and three parts blind,
He cannot catch Thy Commandments. He cannot read Thy Mind.
Oh, leave him not in his loneliness; nor make him that kitten's scorn.

He has had none other God than Thee since the year that he was born!

Lord, look down on Thy Servant! Bad things have come to pass,
There is no heat in the midday sun nor health in the wayside grass.
His bones are full of an old disease—his torments run and increase.
Lord, make haste with Thy Lightnings and grant him a quick release!

'TEEM': A TREASURE-HUNTER

There's a gentleman of France—better met by choice than chance,
Where there's time to turn aside and space to flee—
He is born and bred and made for the cattle-droving trade,
And they call him Monsieur Bouvier de Brie.
'What—Brie?' 'Yes, Brie.' 'Where those funny cheeses come from?'
'Oui! Oui! Oui!
But his name is great through Gaul as the wisest dog of all,
And France pays high for Bouvier de Brie.'
'De Brie?' 'C'est lui. And, if you read my story,—you will see
What one loyal little heart thought of Life and Love and Art,
And notably of Bouvier de Brie—
"My friend the Vicomte Bouvier de Brie."'

NOTHING could prevent my adored Mother from demanding at once the piece of sugar which was her just reward for every Truffle she found. My revered Father, on the other hand, contented himself with the strict practice of his Art. So soon as that Pierre, our Master, stooped to dig at the spot indicated, my Father moved on to fresh triumphs.

From my Father I inherit my nose, and, perhaps, a touch of genius. From my Mother a practical philosophy without which even Genius is but a bird of one wing.

In appearance? My Parents come of a race built up from remote times on the Gifted of various strains. The fine flower of it to-day is small— of a rich gold, touched with red; pricked and open ears; a broad and receptive brow; eyes of intense but affable outlook, and a Nose in itself an inspiration and unerring guide. Is it any wonder, then, that my Parents stood apart from the generality? Yet I would not make light of those worthy artisans who have to be trained by Persons to the pursuit of Truffles. They are of many stocks and possess many virtues, but not the Nose—that gift which is incommunicable.

Myself? I am not large. At birth, indeed, I was known as The Dwarf; but my achievements early won me the title of The Abbé. It was easy. I do not recall that I was ever trained by any Person. I watched, imitated, and, at need, improved upon, the technique of my Parents among the little thin oaks of my country where the best Truffles are found; and that which to the world seemed a chain of miracles was, for me, as easy as to roll in the dust.

My small feet could walk the sun up and down across the stony hill-crests where we worked. My well-set coat turned wet, wind, and cold, and my size enabled me to be carried, on occasion, in my Master's useful outside pocket.

My companions of those days? At first Pluton and Dis—the solemn, dewlapped, black, mated pair who drew the little wooden cart whence my master dispensed our Truffles at the white Château near our village, and to certain shopkeepers in the Street of the Fountain where the women talk. Those Two of Us were peasants in grain. They made clear to me the significance of the flat round white Pieces, and the Thin Papers, which my Master and his Mate buried beneath the stone by their fireplace. Not only Truffles but all other things, Pluton told me, turn into Pieces or Thin Papers at last.

But my friend of friends; my preceptor, my protector, my life-long admiration; was Monsieur le Vicomte Bouvier de Brie—a Marshal of Bulls whom he controlled in the stony pastures near the cottage. There were many sheep also, with whom neither the Vicomte nor I was concerned. Mutton is bad for the Nose, and, as I have reason to know, for the disposition.

He was of race, too—'born' as I was—and so accepted me when, with the rash abandon of puppyhood, I attached myself to his ear. In place of abolishing me, which he could have done with one of his fore-paws, he lowered me gently between both of them, so that I lay blinking up the gaunt cliff of his chest into his unfathomable eyes, and 'Little bad one!' he said. 'But I prophesy thou wilt go far!'

Here, fenced by those paws, I would repair for my slumbers, to avoid my enemies or to plague him with questions. And, when he went to the Railway Station to receive or despatch more Bulls, I would march beneath his belly, hurling infantile insults at the craven doggerie of the Street of the Fountain. After I was expert in my Art, he would talk to me of his own, breaking off with some thunder of command to a young Bull who presumed to venture too near the woods where our Truffles grow, or descending upon him like hail across walls which his feet scorned to touch.

His strength, his audacity, overwhelmed me. He, on his side, was frankly bewildered by my attainments. 'But how—how, little one, is it done, your business?' I could not convey to him, nor he to me, the mystery of our several Arts. Yet always unweariedly he gave me the fruits of his experience and philosophy.

I recall a day when I had chased a chicken which, for the moment, represented to me a sufficiently gross Bull of Salers. There seemed a possibility of chastisement at the hands of the owner, and I refuged me beneath my friend's neck where he watched in the sun. He listened to my foolish tale, and said, as to himself, 'These Bulls of mine are but beef fitted with noses and tails by which one regulates them. But these black hidden lumps of yours which only such as you can unearth— that is a business beyond me! I should like to add it to my repertoire.'

'And I,' I cried (my second teeth were just pushing), 'I will be a Driver of Bulls!'

'Little one,' he responded with infinite tenderness, 'here is one thing for us both to remember. Outside his Art, an Artist must never dream.'

About my fifteenth month I found myself brother to four who wearied me. At the same time there was a change in my Master's behaviour. Never having had any regard for him, I was the quicker to notice his lack of attention. My Mother, as always, said, 'If it is not something, it is sure to be something else.' My Father simply, 'At all hazards follow your Art. That can never lead to a false scent.'

There came a Person of abominable odours to our cottage, not once but many times. One day my Master worked me in his presence. I demonstrated, through a long day of changing airs, with faultless precision. After supper, my Master's Mate said to him, 'We are sure of at least two good workers for next season—and with a dwarf one never knows. It is far off, that England the man talks of. Finish the affair, Pierril.'

Some Thin Papers passed from hand to hand. The Person then thrust me into his coat-pocket (Ours is not a breed to be shown to all) and there followed for me alternations of light and dark in stink-carts: a period when my world rose and rolled till I was sick; a silence beside lapping water under stars; transfer to another Person whose scent and speech were unintelligible; another flight by stink-cart; a burst of sunrise between hedges; a scent of sheep; violent outcries and rockings: finally, a dissolution of the universe which projected me through a hedge from which I saw my captor lying beneath the stink- cart where a large black-and-white She bit him with devotion.

A ditch led me to the shelter of a culvert. I composed myself within till the light was suddenly blocked out by the head of that very She, who abused me savagely in Lingua canina. [My Father often recommended me never to reply to a strange She.] I was glad when her Master's voice recalled this one to her duties, and I heard the clickety of her flock's feet above my head.

In due time I issued forth to acquaint myself with this world into which I had been launched. It was new in odour and aspect, but with points of likeness to my old one. Clumps of trees fringed close woods and smooth green pastures; and, at the bottom of a shallow basin crowned with woodland, stood a white Château even larger than the one to which Pluton and Dis used to pull their cart.

I kept me among the trees, and was congratulating my Nose on its recovery from the outrageous assaults it had suffered during my journeys, when there came to it the unmistakable aroma of Truffles— not, indeed, the strawberry-scented ones of my lost world, but like enough to throw me into my working-pose.

I took wind, and followed up my line. I was not deceived. There were Truffles of different sorts in their proper places under those thick trees. My Mother's maxim had proved its truth. This was evidently the 'something else' of which she had spoken; and I felt myself again my own equal. As I worked amid the almost familiar odours it seemed to me that all that had overtaken me had not happened, and that at any moment I should meet Pluton and Dis with our cart. But they came not. Though I called they did not come.

A far-off voice interrupted me, with menace. I recognised it for that of the boisterous She of my culvert, and was still.

After cautious circuits I heard the sound of a spade, and in a wooded hollow saw a Person flattening earth round a pile of wood, heaped to make charcoal. It was a business I had seen often.

My Nose assured me that the Person was authentically a peasant and (I recalled the memory later) had not handled One of Us within the time that such a scent would hang on him. My Nose, further, recorded that he was imbued with the aromas proper to his work and was, also, kind, gentle, and equable in temperament. (You Persons wonder that All of Us know your moods before you yourselves realise them? Be well sure that every shade of his or her character, habit, or feeling cries itself aloud in a Person's scent. No more than We All can deceive Each Other can You Persons deceive Us—though We pretend—We pretend—to believe!)

His coat lay on a bank. When he drew from it bread and cheese, I produced myself. But I had been so long at gaze, that my shoulder, bruised in transit through the hedge, made me fall. He was upon me at once and, with strength equal to his gentleness, located my trouble. Evidently—though the knowledge even then displeased me—he knew how We should be handled.

I submitted to his care, ate the food he offered, and, reposing in the crook of his mighty arm, was borne to a small cottage where he bathed my hurt, set water beside me and returned to his charcoal. I slept, lulled by the cadence of his spade and the bouquet of natural scents in the cottage which included all those I was used to, except garlic and, strangely, Truffles.

I was roused by the entry of a She-Person who moved slowly and coughed. There was on her (I speak now as We speak) the Taint of the Fear—of that Black Fear which bids Us throw up our noses and lament. She laid out food. The Person of the Spade entered. I fled to his knee. He showed me to the Girl-Person's dull eyes. She caressed my head, but the chill of her hand increased the Fear. He set me on his knees, and they talked in the twilight.

Presently, their talk nosed round hidden flat Pieces and Thin Papers. The tone was so exactly that of my Master and his Mate that I expected they would lift up the hearthstone. But theirs was in the chimney, whence the Person drew several white Pieces, which he gave to the Girl. I argued from this they had admitted me to their utmost intimacy and—I confess it—I danced like a puppy. My reward was their mirth— his specially. When the Girl laughed she coughed. But his voice warmed and possessed me before I knew it.

After night was well fallen, they went out and prepared a bed on a cot in the open, sheltered only by a large faggot-stack. The Girl disposed herself to sleep there, which astonished me. (In my lost world out- sleeping is not done, except when Persons wish to avoid Forest Guards.) The Person of the Spade then set a jug of water by the bed and, turning to reenter the house, delivered a long whistle. It was answered across the woods by the unforgettable voice of the old She of my culvert. I inserted myself at once between, and a little beneath, some of the more robust faggots.

On her silent arrival the She greeted the Girl with extravagant affection and fawned beneath her hand, till the coughings closed in uneasy slumber. Then, with no more noise than the moths of the night, she quested for me in order, she said, to tear out my throat.

'Ma Tante,' I replied placidly from within my fortress, 'I do not doubt you could save yourself the trouble by swallowing me alive. But, first, tell me what I have done.' 'That there is My Bone,' was the reply. It was enough! (Once in my life I had seen poor honest Pluton stand like a raging wolf between his Pierril, whom he loved, and a Forest Guard.) We use that word seldom and never lightly. Therefore, I answered, 'I assure you she is not mine. She gives me the Black Fear.'

You know how We cannot deceive Each Other? The She accepted my statement; at the same time reviling me for my lack of appreciation—a crookedness of mind not uncommon among elderly Shes.

To distract her, I invited her to tell me her history. It appeared that the Girl had nursed her through some early distemper. Since then, the She had divided her life between her duties among sheep by day and watching, from the First Star till Break of Light, over the Girl, who, she said, also suffered from a slight distemper. This had been her existence, her joy and her devotion long before I was born. Demanding nothing more, she was prepared to back her single demand by slaughter.

Once, in my second month, when I would have run away from a very fierce frog, my friend the Vicomte told me that, at crises, it is best to go forward. On a sudden impulse I emerged from my shelter and sat beside her. There was a pause of life and death during which I had leisure to contemplate all her teeth. Fortunately, the Girl waked to drink. The She crawled to caress the hand that set down the jug, and waited till the breathing resumed. She came back to me—I had not stirred—with blazing eyes. 'How can you dare this?' she said. 'But why not?' I answered. 'If it is not something, it is sure to be something else.' Her fire and fury passed. 'To whom do you say it! 'she assented. 'There is always something else to fear—not for myself but for My Bone yonder.'

Then began a conversation unique, I should imagine, even among Ourselves. My old, unlovely, savage Aunt, as I shall henceforth call her, was eaten alive with fears for the Girl—not so much on account of her distemper, but because of Two She-Persons-Enemies—whom she described to me minutely by Eye and Nose—one like a Ferret, the other like a Goose.

These, she said, meditated some evil to the Girl against which my Aunt and the Girl's Father, the Person of the Spade, were helpless. The Two Enemies carried about with them certain papers, by virtue of which the Girl could be taken away from the cottage and my Aunt's care, precisely as she had seen sheep taken out of her pasture by Persons with papers, and driven none knew whither.

The Enemies would come at intervals to the cottage in daytime (when my Aunt's duty held her with the sheep) and always they left behind them the Taint of misery and anxiety. It was not that she feared the Enemies personally. She feared nothing except a certain Monsieur The- Law who, I understood later, cowed even her.

Naturally I sympathised. I did not know this gentilhommier de Loire, but I knew Fear. Also, the Girl was of the same stock as He who had fed and welcomed me and Whose voice had reassured. My Aunt suddenly demanded if I purposed to take up my residence with them. I would have detailed to her my adventures. She was acutely uninterested in them all except so far as they served her purposes, which she explained. She would allow me to live on condition that I reported to her, nightly beside the faggot-stack, all I had seen or heard or suspected of every action and mood of the Girl during the day; any arrival of the Enemies, as she called them; and whatever I might gather from their gestures and tones. In other words I was to spy for her as Those of Us who accompany the Forest Guards spy for their detestable Masters.

I was not disturbed. (I had had experience of the Forest Guard.) Still there remained my dignity and something which I suddenly felt was even more precious to me. 'Ma Tante,' I said, 'what I do depends not on you but on My Bone in the cottage there.' She understood. 'What is there on Him,' she said, 'to draw you?' 'Such things are like Truffles,' was my answer. 'They are there or they are not there.' 'I do not know what "Truffles" may be,' she snapped. 'He has nothing useful to me except that He, too, fears for my Girl. At any rate your infatuation for Him makes you more useful as an aid to my plans.' 'We shall see,' said I. 'But—to talk of affairs of importance—do you seriously mean that you have no knowledge of Truffles?' She was convinced that I mocked her. 'Is it,' she demanded, 'some lapdog's trick?' She said this of Truffles—of my Truffles

The impasse was total. Outside of the Girl on the cot and her sheep (for I can testify that, with them, she was an artist) the square box of my Aunt's head held not one single thought. My patience forsook me, but not my politeness. 'Cheer-up, old one!' I said. 'An honest heart outweighs many disadvantages of ignorance and low birth.'...

And She? I thought she would have devoured me in my hair! When she could speak, she made clear that she was 'born'—entirely soof a breed mated and trained since the days of the First Shepherd. In return I explained that I was a specialist in the discovery of delicacies which the genius of my ancestors had revealed to Persons since the First Person first scratched in the first dirt.

She did not believe me—nor do I pretend that I had been entirely accurate in my genealogy—but she addressed me henceforth as 'My Nephew.'

Thus that wonderful night passed, with the moths, the bats, the owls, the sinking moon, and the varied respirations of the Girl. At sunrise a call broke out from beyond the woods. My Aunt vanished to her day's office. I went into the house and found Him lacing one gigantic boot. Its companion lay beside the hearth. I brought it to Him (I had seen my Father do as much for that Pierrounet my Master).

He was loudly pleased. He patted my head, and when the Girl entered, told her of my exploit. She called me to be caressed, and, though the Black Taint upon her made me cringe, I came. She belonged to Him—as at that moment I realised that I did.

Here began my new life. By day I accompanied Him to His charcoal—sole guardian of His coat and the bread and cheese on the bank, or, remembering my Aunt's infatuation, fluctuated between the charcoal- mound and the house to spy upon the Girl, when she was not with Him. He was all that I desired—in the sound of His solid tread; His deep but gentle voice; the sympathetic texture and scent of His clothes; the safe hold of His hand when He would slide me into His great outer pocket and carry me through the far woods where He dealt secretly with rabbits. Like peasants, who are alone more than most Persons, He talked aloud to himself, and presently to me, asking my opinion of the height of a wire from the ground.

My devotion He accepted and repaid from the first. My Art he could by no means comprehend. For, naturally, I followed my Art as every Artist must, even when it is misunderstood. If not, he comes to preoccupy himself mournfully with his proper fleas.

My new surroundings; the larger size and closer spacing of the oaks; the heavier nature of the soils; the habits of the lazy wet winds—a hundred considerations which the expert takes into account—demanded changes and adjustments of my technique...My reward? I found and brought Him Truffles of the best. I nosed them into His hand. I laid them on the threshold of the cottage and they filled it with their fragrance. He and the Girl thought that I amused myself, and would throw—throw!—them for me to retrieve, as though they had been stones and...uppy! What more could I do? The scent over that ground was lost.

But the rest was happiness, tempered with vivid fears when we were apart lest, if the wind blew beyond moderation, a tree might fall and crush Him; lest when He worked late He might disappear into one of those terrible river pits so common in the world whence I had come, and be lost without trace. There was no peril I did not imagine for Him till I could hear His feet walking securely on sound earth long before the Girl had even suspected. Thus my heart was light in spite of the nightly conferences with my formidable Aunt, who linked her own dismal apprehensions to every account that I rendered of the Girl's day-life and actions. For some cause or other, the Two Enemies had not appeared since my Aunt had warned me against them, and there was less of Fear in the house. Perhaps, as I once hinted to my Aunt, owing to my presence.

It was an unfortunate remark. I should have remembered her gender. She attacked me, that night, on a new scent, bidding me observe that she herself was decorated with a Collar of Office which established her position before all the world. I was about to compliment her, when she observed, in the low even tone of detachment peculiar to Shes of age, that, unless I were so decorated, not only was I outside the Law (that Person of whom, I might remember, she had often spoken) but could not be formally accepted into any household.

How, then, I demanded, might I come by this protection? In her own case, she said, the Collar was hers by right as a Preceptress of Sheep. To procure a Collar for me would be a matter of Pieces or even of Thin Papers, from His chimney. (I recalled poor Pluton's warning that everything changes at last into such things.) If He chose to give of His Pieces for my Collar, my civil status would be impregnable. Otherwise, having no business or occupation, I lived, said my Aunt, like the rabbits—by favour and accident.

'But, ma Tante,' I cried, 'I have the secret of an Art beyond all others.'

'That is not understood in these parts,' she replied. 'You have told me of it many times, but I do not believe. What a pity it is not rabbits! You are small enough to creep down their burrows. But these precious things of yours under the ground which no one but you can find—it is absurd.'

'It is an absurdity, then, which fills Persons' chimney-places with Pieces and Thin Papers. Listen, ma Tante!' I all but howled. 'The world I came from was stuffed with things underground which all Persons desired. This world here is also rich in them, but I—I alone—can bring them to light!'

She repeated acridly, 'Here is not there. It should have been rabbits.'

I turned to go. I was at the end of my forces.

'You talk too much of the world whence you came,' my Aunt sneered. 'Where is that world?'

'I do not know,' I answered miserably and crawled under my faggots. As a matter of routine, when my report had been made to my Aunt, I would take post on the foot of His bed where I should be available in case of bandits. But my Aunt's words had barred that ever-open door.

My suspicions worked like worms in my system. If He chose, He could kick me off on to the floor—beyond sound of His desired voice—into the rabid procession of fears and flights whence He had delivered me. Whither, then, should I go?...There remained only my lost world where Persons knew the value of Truffles and of Those of Us who could find them. I would seek that world!

With this intention, and a bitterness in my belly as though I had mouthed a toad, I came out after dawn and fled to the edge of the woods through which He and I had wandered so often. They were bounded by a tall stone wall, along which I quested for an opening. I found none till I reached a small house beside shut gates. Here an officious One of Us advanced upon me with threats. I was in no case to argue or even to expostulate. I hastened away and attacked the wall again at another point.

But after a while, I found myself back at the house of the Officious One. I recommenced my circuit, but—there was no end to that Wall. I remembered crying aloud to it in hope it might fall down and pass me through. I remember appealing to the Vicomte to come to my aid. I remember a flight of big black birds, calling the very name of my lost world—'Aa—or'—above my head. But soon they scattered in all directions. Only the Wall continued to continue, and I blindly at its foot. Once a She-Person stretched out her hand towards me. I fled—as I fled from an amazed rabbit who, like myself, existed by favour and accident.

Another Person coming upon me threw stones. This turned me away from the Wall and so broke its attraction. I subsided into an aimless limp of hours, until some woods that seemed familiar received me into their shades...

I found me at the back of the large white Château in the hollow, which I had seen only once, far off, on the first day of my arrival in this world. I looked down through bushes on to ground divided by strips of still water and stone. Here were birds, bigger than turkeys, with enormous voices and tails which they raised one against the other, while a white-haired She-Person dispensed them food from a pan she held between sparkling hands. My Nose told me that she was unquestionably of race-descended from champion strains. I would have crawled nearer, but the greedy birds forbade. I retreated uphill into the woods, and, moved by I know not what agonies of frustration and bewilderment, threw up my head and lamented.

The harsh imperative call of my Aunt cut through my self-pity. I found her on duty in pastures still bounded by that Wall which encircled my world. She charged me at once with having some disreputable affair, and, for its sake, deserting my post with the Girl. I could but pant. Seeing, at last, my distress, she said, 'Have you been seeking that lost world of yours?' Shame closed my mouth. She continued, in softer tones, 'Except when it concerns My Bone, do not take all that I say at full-fang. There are others as foolish as you. Wait my return.'

She left me with an affectation, almost a coquetry, of extreme fatigue. To her charge had been added a new detachment of sheep who wished to escape. They had scattered into separate crowds, each with a different objective and a different speed. My Aunt, keeping the high ground, allowed them to disperse, till her terrible voice, thrice lifted, brought them to halt. Then, in one long loop of flight, my Aunt, a dumb fury lying wide on their flank, swept down with a certainty, a speed, and a calculation which almost reminded me of my friend the Vicomte. Those diffuse and errant imbeciles reunited and inclined away from her in a mob of mixed smells and outcries—to find themselves exquisitely penned in an angle of the fence, my

Aunt, laid flat at full length, facing them! One after another their heads dropped and they resumed their eternal business of mutton-making.

My Aunt came back, her affectation of decrepitude heightened to heighten her performance. And who was I, an Artist also, to mock her?

'You wonder why my temper is not of the bluntest?' she said. 'You could not have done that!'

'But at least I can appreciate it,' I cried. 'It was superb! It was unequalled! It was faultless! You did not even nip one of them.'

'With sheep that is to confess failure,' she said. 'Do you, then, gnaw your Truffles?' It was the first time that she had ever admitted their existence! My genuine admiration, none the worse for a little flattery, opened her heart. She spoke of her youthful triumphs at sheep—herding expositions; of rescues of lost lambs, or incapable mothers found reversed in ditches. Oh, she was all an Artist, my thin-flanked, haggard-eyed Aunt by enforced adoption. She even let me talk of the Vicomte!

Suddenly (the shadows had stretched) she leaped, with a grace I should never have suspected, on to a stone wall and stood long at far gaze. 'Enough of this nonsense,' she said brutally. 'You are rested now. Get to your work. If you could see, my Nephew, you would observe the Ferret and the Goose walking there, three fields distant. They have come again for My Bone. They will keep to the path made for Persons. Go at once to the cottage before they arrive and—do what you can to harass them. Run—run—mountebank of a yellow imbecile that you are!'

I turned on my tail, as We say, and took the direct line through my well-known woods at my utmost speed since her orders dispatched me without loss of dignity towards my heart's one desire. And I was received by Him, and by the Girl with unfeigned rapture. They passed me from one to the other like the rarest of Truffles; rebuked me, not too severely, for my long absence; felt me for possible injuries from traps; brought me bread and milk, which I sorely needed; and by a hundred delicate attentions showed me the secure place I occupied in their hearts. I gave my dignity to the cats, and it is not too much to say that we were all engaged in a veritable pas de trois when a shadow fell across our threshold and the Two Enemies most rudely entered!

I conceived, and gave vent to, instant detestation which, for a while, delayed their attack. When it came, He and the Girl accepted it as yoked oxen receive the lash across the eyes—with the piteous dignity which Earth, having so little to give them, bestows upon her humbles. Like oxen, too, they backed side by side and pressed closer together. I renewed my comminations from every angle as I saw how these distracted my adversaries. They then pointed passionately to me and my pan of bread and milk which joy had prevented me from altogether emptying. Their tongues I felt were foul with reproach.

At last He spoke. He mentioned my name more than once, but always (I could tell in my defence. The Girl backed His point. I assisted with— and it was something—all that I had ever heard in my lost world from the sans-kennailerie of the Street of the Fountain. The Enemies renewed the charge. Evidently my Aunt was right. Their plan was to take the Girl away in exchange for pieces of paper. I saw the Ferret wave a paper beneath His nose. He shook His head and launched that peasant's 'No,' which is one in all languages.

Here I applauded vehemently, continuously, monotonously, on a key which, also, I had learned in the Street of the Fountain. Nothing could have lived against it. The Enemies threatened, I could feel, some prodigious action or another; but at last they marched out of our presence. I escorted them to the charcoal-heap—the limit of our private domain—in a silence charged with possibilities for their thick ankles.

I returned to find my Two sunk in distress, but upon my account. I think they feared I might run away again, for they shut the door.

They frequently and tenderly repeated my name, which, with them, was 'Teem.' Finally He took a Thin Paper from the chimney-piece, slid me into His outside pocket and walked swiftly to the Village, which I had never smelt before.

In a place where a She-Person was caged behind bars, He exchanged the Thin Paper for one which he laid under my nose, saying 'Teem! Look! This is Licence-and-Law all-right!' In yet another place, I was set down before a Person who exhaled a grateful flavour of dried skins. My neck was then encircled by a Collar bearing a bright badge of office. All Persons round me expressed admiration and said 'Lor!' many times. On our return through the Village I stretched my decorated neck out of His pocket, like one of the gaudy birds at the Château, to impress Those of Us who might be abroad that I was now under full protection of Monsieur Le Law (whoever he might be), and thus the equal of my exacting Aunt.

That night, by the Girl's bed, my Aunt was at her most difficult. She cut short my history of my campaign, and cross-examined me coldly as to what had actually passed. Her interpretations were not cheering. She prophesied our Enemies would return, more savage for having been checked. She said that when they mentioned my name (as I have told you) it was to rebuke Him for feeding me, a vagabond, on good bread and milk, when I did not, according to Monsieur Law, belong to Him. (She herself, she added, had often been shocked by His extravagance in this regard.) I pointed out that my Collar now disposed of inconvenient questions. So much she ungraciously conceded, but—I had described the scene to her—argued that He had taken the Thin Paper out of its hiding-place because I had cajoled Him with my 'lapdog's tricks,' and that, in default of that Paper, He would go without food, as well as without what he burned under His nose, which to Him would be equally serious.

I was aghast. 'But, Ma Tante,' I pleaded, 'show me—make me any way to teach Him that the earth on which He walks so loftily can fill His chimneys with Thin Papers, and I promise you that She shall eat chicken!' My evident sincerity—perhaps, too, the finesse of my final appeal—shook her. She mouthed a paw in thought.

'You have shown Him those wonderful underground-things of yours?' she resumed.

'But often. And to your Girl also. They thought they were stones to throw. It is because of my size that I am not taken seriously.' I would have lamented, but she struck me down. Her Girl was coughing.

'Be silent, unlucky that you are! Have you shown your Truffles, as you call them, to anyone else?'

'Those Two are all I have ever met in this world, my Aunt.'

'That was true till yesterday,' she replied. 'But at the back of the Château—this afternoon—eh?' (My friend the Vicomte was right when he warned me that all elderly Shes have six ears and ten noses. And the older the more!)

'I saw that Person only from a distance. You know her, then, my Aunt?'

'If I know Her! She met me once when I was lamed by thorns under my left heel-pad. She stopped me. She took them out. She also put her hand on my head.'

'Alas, I have not your charms!' I riposted.

'Listen, before my temper snaps, my Nephew. She has returned to her Château. Lay one of those things that you say you find, at her feet. I do not credit your tales about them, but it is possible that She may. She is of race. She knows all. She may make you that way for which you ask so loudly. It is only a chance. But, if it succeeds, and

My Bone does not eat the chickens you have promised her, I will, for sure, tear out your throat.'

'My Aunt,' I replied, 'I am infinitely obliged. You have, at least, shown me a way. What a pity you were born with so many thorns under your tongue!' And I fled to take post at the foot of His bed, where I slept vigorously—for I had lived that day!—till time to bring Him His morning boots.

We then went to our charcoal. As official Guardian of the Coat I permitted myself no excursions till He was busied stopping the vents of little flames on the flanks of the mound. Then I moved towards a patch of ground which I had noted long ago. On my way, a chance of the air told me that the Born One of the Château was walking on the verge of the wood. I fled to my patch, which was even more fruitful than I had thought. I had unearthed several Truffles when the sound of her tread hardened on the bare ground beneath the trees. Selecting my largest and ripest, I bore it reverently towards her, dropped it in her path, and took a pose of humble devotion. Her Nose informed her before her eyes. I saw it wrinkle and sniff deliciously. She stooped and with sparkling hands lifted my gift to smell. Her sympathetic appreciation emboldened me to pull the fringe of her clothes in the direction of my little store exposed beneath the oak. She knelt and, rapturously inhaling their aroma, transferred them to a small basket on her arm. (All Born Ones bear such baskets when they walk upon their own earths.)

Here He called my name. I replied at once that I was coming, but that matters of the utmost importance held me for the moment. We moved on together, the Born One and I, and found Him beside His coat setting apart for me my own bread and cheese. We lived, we two, each always in the other's life!

I had often seen that Pierrounet my Master, who delivered me to strangers, uncover and bend at the side-door of the Château in my lost world over yonder. At no time was he beautiful. But He—My Own Bone to me!—though He too was uncovered, stood beautifully erect and as a peasant of race should bear himself when He and His are not being tortured by Ferrets or Geese. For a short time, He and the Born One did not concern themselves with me. They were obviously of old acquaintance. She spoke; she waved her sparkling hands; she laughed. He responded gravely, at dignified ease, like my friend the Vicomte. Then I heard my name many times. I fancy He may have told her something of my appearance in this world. (We peasants do not tell all to any one.) To prove to her my character, as He conceived it, He threw a stone. With as much emphasis as my love for Him allowed, I signified that this game of lapdogs was not mine. She commanded us to return to the woods. There He said to me as though it were some question of His magnificent boots, 'Seek, Teem! Find, Teem!' and waved His arms at random. He did not know! Even then, My Bone did not know!

But I—I was equal to the occasion! Without unnecessary gesture; stifling the squeaks of rapture that rose in my throat; coldly, almost, as my Father, I made point after point, picked up my lines and worked them (His attendant spade saving me the trouble of digging) till the basket was full. At this juncture the Girl—they were seldom far apart—appeared with all the old miseries on her face, and, behind her (I had been too occupied with my Art, or I should have yelled on their scent) walked the Two Enemies!

They had not spied us up there among the trees, for they rated her all the way to the charcoal-heap. Our Born One descended upon them softly as a mist through which shine the stars, and greeted them in the voice of a dove out of summer foliage. I held me still. She needed no aid, that one! They grew louder and more loud; she increasingly more suave. They flourished at her one of their detestable papers which she received as though it had been all the Trufes in the world. They talked of Monsieur Le Law. From her renewed smiles I understood that he, too, had the honour of her friendship. They continued to talk of him...Then...she abolished them! How? Speaking with the utmost reverence of both, she reminded me of my friend the Vicomte disentangling an agglomeration of distracted, and therefore dangerous, beefs at the Railway Station. There was the same sage turn of the head, the same almost invisible stiffening of the shoulders, the very same small voice out of the side of the mouth, saying 'I charge myself with this.' And then—and then—those insupportable offspring of a jumped-up gentilhommier were transformed into amiable and impressed members of their proper class, giving ground slowly at first, but finally evaporating—yes, evaporating—like bad smells—in the direction of the world whence they had intruded.

During the relief that followed, the Girl wept and wept and wept. Our Born One led her to the cottage and consoled. We showed her our bed beside the faggots and all our other small dispositions, including a bottle out of which the Girl was used to drink. (I tasted once some that had been spilt. It was like unfresh fish—fit only for cats.) She saw, she heard, she considered all. Calm came at her every word. She would have given Him some Pieces, in exchange, I suppose, for her filled basket. He pointed to me to show that it was my work. She repeated most of the words she had employed before—my name among them—because one must explain many times to a peasant who desires not to comprehend. At last He took the Pieces.

Then my Born One stooped down to me beside His foot and said, in the language of my lost world, 'Knowest thou, Teem, that this is all thy work? Without thee we can do nothing. Knowest thou, my little dear Teem?' If I knew! Had He listened to me at the first the situation would have been regularised half a season before. Now I could fill his chimney-places as my Father had filled that of that disgusting Pierrounet. Logically, of course, I should have begun a fresh demonstration of my Art in proof of my zeal for the interests of my famille. But I did not. Instead, I ran—I rolled—I leaped—I cried aloud—I fawned at their knees What would you? It was hairless, toothless sentiment, but it had the success of a hurricane! They accepted me as though I had been a Person—and He more unreservedly than any of them. It was my supreme moment!

I have at last reduced my famille to the Routine which is indispensable to the right-minded among Us. For example: At intervals He and I descend to the Château with our basket of Truffles for our Born One. If she is there she caresses me. If elsewhere, her basket pursues her in a stink-cart. So does, also, her Chef, a well-scented Person and, I can testify, an Artist. This, I understand, is our exchange for the right to exploit for ourselves all other Truffles that I may find inside the Great Wall. These we dispense to another stink-cart, filled with delightful comestibles, which waits for us regularly on the stink-cart-road by the House of the Gate where the Officious One pursued me. We are paid into the hand (trust us peasants!) in Pieces or Papers, while I stand guard against bandits.

As a result, the Girl has now a wooden-roofed house of her own—open at one side and capable of being turned round against winds by His strong one hand. Here she arranges the bottles from which she drinks, and here comes—but less and less often—a dry Person of mixed odours, who applies his ear at the end of a stick, to her thin back. Thus, and owing to the chickens which, as I promised my Aunt, she eats, the Taint of her distemper diminishes. My Aunt denies that it ever existed, but her infatuation—have I told you?—has no bounds! She has been given honourable demission from her duties with sheep and has frankly installed herself in the Girl's outside bed-house, which she does not encourage me to enter. I can support that. I too have My Bone...

Only it comes to me, as it does to most of Us who live so swiftly, to dream in my sleep. Then I return to my lost world—to the whistling, dry-leaved, thin oaks that are not these giant ones—to the stony little hillsides and treacherous river-pits that are not these secure pastures—to the sharp scents that are not these scents—to the companionship of poor Pluton and Dis—to the Street of the Fountain up which marches to meet me, as when I was a rude little puppy, my friend, my protector, my earliest adoration, Monsieur le Vicomte Bouvier de Brie.

At this point always, I wake; and not till I feel His foot beneath the bedderie, and hear His comfortable breathing, does my lost world cease to bite...

Oh, wise and well-beloved guardian and playmate of my youth—it is true—it is true, as thou didst warn me—Outside his Art an Artist must never dream!

THE END